Fated Lies

Ella Miles

LIES SERIES

Lies We Share: A Prologue

Vicious Lies
Desperate Lies
Fated Lies
Cruel Lies
Dangerous Lies
Endless Lies

PROLOGUE
LIESEL

I'VE ALWAYS WONDERED what my fate would be.

Would I someday fall in love or would my life be filled with hating enemies?

Would I spend my life alone or with a group of close friends to call family?

Would I marry or enjoy the single life?

Would I have kids or be focused on my career?

Would I find someone to love or spend my life regretting having loved and lost?

Would I live long or die quick?

After living as long as I have, my fate isn't rosy. I'm destined to suffer every agony life has to offer—to die young.

For a long time, I thought I could change my fate. That I could take on the world and win.

I know better now. My fate is not to love. It's not even to survive. My fate is to protect him...

1

LANGSTON

I'VE SEEN death so many times that it's as routine as breathing for me. Usually, death occurs at my hand.

Not this time.

This time it's happening at the hand of a woman I thought would never see murder. I thought if I did the killing, it would keep her pure, innocent, and intact.

I was wrong.

Liesel Dunn is just as savage as I am. She can kill in cold blood as easily as I can, and that's terrifying. There is no stopping her now. Now she'll come for every single one of us.

Liesel pulls the trigger, and my world stops.

I didn't think she had it in her. I really didn't think she did. But the tears, combined with her pulling the trigger on one of my best friends, one of the only people I love, has me convinced.

Fuck...

Everything happens in slow motion and at double speed.

My lungs and heart slow down so much that my body is basically a standing corpse, not getting enough oxygen or blood. While Siren falling to the ground happens so fast that I don't even notice where the bullet hits her.

Siren can't be dead.

No.

There is no way I'll believe it. I've seen death. I've seen close friends 'die,' but they turned out to be fine. So even though I'm watching Siren drop with my own eyes, it doesn't mean she's dead.

I drag my eyes to Siren's chest. Her chest is rising. She's still alive—for now.

I want to run to Siren. To stop her suffering, to help her stay alive, but Maxwell still has a gun pointed at me. Liesel still has a gun on Siren. If she hasn't already killed her, another shot could. I have to make my next move carefully.

It's impossible to think, though. All I can feel is Liesel's pain. Unbearable, devastating, just lost the love of her life kind of pain.

She really did love Waylon.

That suffocates me. My own airway begins to strangle me with her tears, her agony pulsing off her in waves. It's the purest thing I've ever felt.

How could she have loved him? It doesn't make sense to me. Nothing I noticed between her and Waylon told me she loved him.

Except she fucked him like she loved him. She was going to marry him. She wouldn't take his money. She wanted to be his equal. *Maybe I was very wrong about her and Waylon's relationship? Maybe he didn't hurt her? Maybe he was trying to protect her from me?*

I can't process it. I'm overwhelmed by her pain and mine. We are two broken hearts who just lost the love of our lives.

No—I didn't lose Siren, not yet. I can still save her.

Zeke has the exact same idea and is hopping in his chair

with his legs still tied together, but his arms free toward Siren and Liesel.

I take the moment to disarm Maxwell as Zeke tackles Liesel and wrestles the gun away from her. She doesn't put up much of a fight. She's too broken—completely heartbroken.

The threat is over. Zeke and I both have the guns.

I return my gaze to Liesel as Zeke aims the gun at her.

"This is for Siren," Zeke says.

My heart stops.

Zeke should get to kill Liesel for what she just did to Siren. Whether or not Siren dies, Liesel deserves it—not to mention her other crime...

I turn away.

I can't watch.

But suddenly my body is flying. I'm not thinking straight. I'm not thinking at all. I run as fast as I can, knowing that I'm fast enough. There is nothing that could ever stop me from getting to Zeke, from stopping him from hurting Liesel.

"Get the fuck off me. She deserves to die," Zeke yells, a man who hasn't yet accepted what has happened to the love of his life.

"Put the damn gun down, Zeke," I say as I point my gun at him.

I won't let him hurt Liesel, my huntress. He can't hurt her. He can't kill her.

"No—no more games. She dies today, not however many months you want to wait to get answers. She'll never give them to you. She dies today."

Liesel is ignoring our fight. She doesn't give a damn if she dies or not. She's drowning in her own tears. She would probably prefer us to kill her and make the pain stop.

"Liesel isn't dying today," I say, still holding onto Zeke's back. Zeke is twice the size of me. Physically, he's stronger.

The only way to beat him is to outsmart him, which in his grief just might be possible. But he's not the only one grieving. My brain isn't functioning at the moment.

Boom.

The gun goes off.

No.

No, no, no...

I look over at Liesel. She's still alive. I don't see any blood. I follow her gaze to my leg, and that's when I see my own blood spilling out.

I exhale, thankful the bullet hit me. No one else I love will die.

I can't feel the physical pain. All I can feel is the heartbreak.

Zeke sees the blood, and finally, I'm able to wrestle the gun from him.

"Why did you stop me?" Zeke whispers.

My heart clenches. Because I care about Liesel more than I will ever admit out loud. More than I care about Siren. More than one can care about another person. And yet, I still want to kill her for what she's done.

My plan failed, in so many fucking ways. I need to rethink everything when it comes to Liesel. There are so many pieces that I'm missing. At least now I have some of the truth. I need to lay it all out like an unsolved crime to figure out the rest of her lies.

"Go to Siren. She needs you right now," I tell Zeke before he tries to grab the gun from me again.

Zeke slinks on the ground to where Siren lies. I think he was too afraid to go to her. Too afraid that he might find her dead.

I watch as he lifts her bloodied head into his large lap with his rough hands. He strokes her face and whispers something into her ear.

Her chest is still rising and falling.

Siren is still alive.

She has to be my first priority. I have to make sure she's alive. That's all that matters right now. I need to keep my family intact and alive. The rest I'll figure out later.

I look to Maxwell, who isn't much of a bodyguard unarmed.

I hold up one of the guns I now possess and aim it at him. He doesn't even flinch. He's prepared to die.

Interesting.

"Get Liesel off the boat—now. There is a small speedboat at the back. Take it."

Maxwell nods, and then he calmly walks toward Liesel. I keep the gun aimed at him, unsure if he's going to try something stupid.

He bends down in front of Liesel, who is in an entirely different world. She has no tears left; there are just dry streaks on her cheeks where her tears once were. But her crying won't be enough to get her torment out. It will live with her for a long time.

I've felt the death of someone I loved before. It never leaves you. I feel for Liesel, I do. But right now, I have to make sure that I don't have to endure the same level of pain with Siren.

Maxwell says something to her that I can't hear. She doesn't react.

He carefully slips his arms underneath her, afraid that she's going to lash out or do something to get them both killed.

He lifts her up, cradling her honeymoon-style.

I continue to aim the gun at him, as my heart explodes, watching Liesel so vulnerable in another man's arms and not going to her. *How did things get so fucked up? How did the girl I used to do anything to protect become this?*

Because I failed to protect her from the danger.

Maxwell carries Liesel past me, and I don't turn to look at her. I pocket the gun, and then I turn back to Zeke and Siren. She's still breathing, but there is so much fucking blood. It's all over Zeke's lap.

This isn't something that Zeke and I can fix. Only the best surgeon in the world, with the help of a miracle, would be able to save Siren.

I run up to the top deck and wave Enzo down in the helicopter, knowing that's the fastest way to get Siren to shore.

Finally, I'm able to feel the rage for the possibility that Siren might die.

That can't happen.

I turn, just as I see Maxwell and Liesel disappear out of sight.

In a split second, I've changed my mind. Liesel has to die for what she did to Siren and for what she did before. I can't wait much longer to kill her.

"One month."

2

LIESEL

MY STOMACH HEAVES up and then slams down.

Over and over.

That's what rough waves will do to you—make you lose your stomach until you eventually vomit.

Losing someone you love will also do it.

I'm sure I'm in shock. That's what's happening. It's why I can't feel anything. I'm numb to touch, to motion, to the sea salt splashing in my face.

"Twenty more minutes," I hear Maxwell say, but his voice sounds far off in the distance. I can hear him, but his words don't matter.

I just lost everything.

I lost everything I've ever cared about. Everything I've ever fought for. Everything I've ever considered loving—I lost it all.

I've lost a lot in my life.

My parents.

My innocence.

My child.

Langston.

But this time—it's different. This time I had a chance to love what I lost. This time I fought to try and save it. And I lost.

I need to shut out the pain. I need to push it away so that I can focus on what I need to do next, but I can't. It's in every muscle, bone, and nerve in my body. There is no hiding from it. It's all I'll ever feel again.

I see the shore in the distance.

I'm going to have to function like a human soon, but all I can focus on is how the waves launch our tiny speed boat into the air and then slam us back down. That's my life. I get one brief moment of happiness, of joy, of positivity—only to have life slam me with the worst thing imaginable.

I don't want anything positive, not anymore. Every good thing has been taken from me. I don't want hope. I don't want love. I reject it all. I will not allow myself to feel anything close to love ever again.

The boat stops.

I look around and see Maxwell tying the boat to the dock.

I should get out, but I can't move. My brain can't even function well enough to tell me to stand. My mouth is incapable of speech. My eyes don't really see beyond the haze.

Maxwell must know that because he doesn't ask me to get out. He doesn't ask what's wrong with me.

After he finishes tying the boat, he climbs back in.

"I'm going to lift you out of this boat and get you in a car. Just tell me if that isn't okay, but otherwise, I don't need you to speak at all if you don't want to." His words are soft and soothing.

How does he know exactly what I need?

I give him the tiniest of nods, and then he once again lifts me gently like I'm a broken doll, and one wrong move would end me. It probably would. That's how fragile I am right now.

He carries me to a car. I don't know how he got a car here, but he did.

He lays me sideways in the backseat before he closes the door. Then he carefully walks to the front seat and starts driving.

He doesn't ask me for a destination, and I honestly don't know where I would tell him. He just drives.

I close my eyes, trying to get a moment to breathe. But all I can see is the blood on my bed, Waylon's lifeless body, and what that means.

The car stops suddenly, my eyes fly open.

Waylon drove me back to my apartment.

"I've got you," he says, lifting me out.

He carries me into the lobby before he realizes he made a mistake.

Flashes blind us as reporters swarm us with their microphones and cameras.

"Jesus," he curses. Maxwell is sweet enough, but he's not the brightest. Of course, the media found out that Waylon is dead. A man running for governor showing up dead in my apartment makes for an excellent story.

"Miss Dunn, were you upset that your fiancé was cheating on you? Is that why you killed him?" one brave journalist asks me.

Maxwell growls. The reporters take the hint and back up half a step, but that's as much room as they give us.

"Maxwell!" Nolan shouts from across the lobby.

Maxwell turns his head as Nolan pushes through the crowd to us. "Take her to my house. We have a whole team setup there. You can't go to her apartment anyway; it's a crime scene."

Nolan looks at me with disappointment, like this is somehow my fault.

Quickly, Maxwell has me out of the lobby and back in the car. This time, Nolan sits in the passenger seat, and they both discuss me like I'm not even here.

"Has she been like this the whole time?" Nolan asks, like he can't believe how weak I am.

"Pretty much. She's completely distraught. But can you blame her? She thought she was going to marry Waylon and spend the rest of her life with him. Cut her a break. No one reacts well in this situation."

"Well, I need her to do a press conference soon," Nolan says.

"Why? Waylon is dead. You don't have a candidate to support anymore. Your job is done."

"My job is far from done," Nolan says.

He's heartless. I don't know what Nolan has planned, but if I didn't know that Langston killed Waylon, Nolan would be my number one suspect. He's up to something—I just don't have the energy to figure out what.

My eyes glaze over as Maxwell drives us away. Building after building passes by. Car after car. Tree after tree. None of it registers. I don't even know where Nolan lives.

I see the city disappearing behind us, and yet, we keep driving.

The car slows as we turn down a car-lined suburban street. I don't know how this is going to help keep me away from the press, but maybe that's not the point. Maybe the point is to force me to talk to the media.

"Pull into the garage," Nolan says.

I exhale a deep breath I've been holding since we turned down the cul-de-sac. I won't have to talk to the press.

I don't pay attention as Maxwell pulls the car into the garage. As soon as he parks, he'll open my door and offer to carry me again, but I'm tired of being carried. I'm tired of relying on someone else. I know better than to trust another man.

As soon as Maxwell stops the car, I open my door and climb out. Nolan opens his door at the same time and walks toward the house door. I follow him inside.

"You okay?" Maxwell catches my arm just before I step inside.

I nod.

Reluctantly, Maxwell lets go of my arm, and I enter the house.

"I'm so sorry about your loss, Mrs. Brown," a woman in a suit comes up to me and says.

I give her a tight nod as I push past her in the hallway and into the kitchen.

Big mistake.

A dozen eyes stare at me, and each pair begins to approach me.

"I just can't believe he's gone. You must be so devastated," a woman in a black dress says, gripping my hands.

I stare down at where she's touching my hand and pull my hands abruptly away before pushing past her.

"I'm Toby Cox, I was working on Mr. Brown's campaign. I'm so sad he's gone. Please, accept my condolences," a man in suit pants and a buttoned-down white shirt with the sleeves rolled up says to me.

I frown at him with my eyes.

Then I let my daggers cut through everyone in the room, warning them to stay the fuck away from me. I'm hurting. I'm in pain. I'm in shock. I'm still reeling from the loss. And these people have the audacity to approach me, to speak to me.

I don't even know these people. They worked with

Waylon on his campaign or in his law office. We aren't friends. We aren't family.

I run out of the room. I don't know where I'm supposed to be staying tonight, and since Nolan hasn't escorted me to a room, I'll take whatever room I want.

I reach the stairs and run up, all the time feeling odd stares from the room.

"Leave her alone. She needs space to mourn. She just lost her fiancé," I hear Maxwell trying to defend me.

I don't care what anyone thinks of me.

And I don't need a man to protect me.

I run down the hallway to the farthest room from the stairs and peer inside. It looks to be an unoccupied guest room.

Thank god.

I open the door and slam it shut behind me. I find a lock on the door.

Perfect.

I lock the door and then walk to the bathroom where a large freestanding white tub sits. I flip the water on, intending to wash the pain away. But as the water runs, I collapse onto the floor and cry.

I've already forgotten how it feels to cry—to let warm, wet tears flow down my cheeks.

So many people came up to me apologizing for my loss, but none of them understand the depth of what I just lost.

Langston won.

I lost.

It's over.

I hope Langston is in as much pain as I am. I hope he's lying on a bathroom floor somewhere crying his eyes out with all hope lost.

But I don't care. Even if he is, he won. He just doesn't know it yet.

3

LANGSTON

I SHED ONE LAST TEAR.

In that tear, I feel everything. Its warmth and wetness fills the corner of my eye, fogging my sight of the ocean from Enzo's balcony. It burns until I finally release it. It starts its quick journey rolling down my cheek until it hits the scruff on my chin. The tear slows and pinballs between each fiber of hair on my face until it reaches the edge of my chin. There it drops onto the deck where my feet stand.

That is the last tear. I've already decided that I can't keep spending my days crying. I need to take action. My tears won't save Siren. They won't protect my children, my wife. They won't make Liesel tell me the truth. They won't put an end to my suffering.

So I stop crying.

I hear footsteps approach. Even though the man is capable of walking without sound, he lets me know he's coming to talk.

I'm not sure I'm ready to talk, not after everything I've been through in the last few weeks, but Enzo Black won't give me a choice. He's one of my best friends. I've known him since we were kids. We've protected each other. He made me filthy rich. He's my brother in every way that matters.

But right now, I don't want to hear his opinion because I already know what it will be. Punish Liesel and then let her go.

Enzo leans on the railing next to me. He's a patient man, more patient than I am. He could wait me out, and I'd start talking.

"Why?" Enzo asks, still staring straight ahead. If he doesn't look at me, maybe I'll answer more honestly. I haven't had many reasons to lie to Enzo or any of my friends, but lately, I find myself lying more than telling the truth.

When I don't answer, Enzo sighs and then turns and looks at me.

I stare back. His eyes are swollen, his dark hair disheveled, and he's wearing sweatpants and a grey hoodie. He looks like he hasn't gotten any more sleep than I have. He doesn't look like a boss; he looks like a broken man.

"Why go after the treasure? Why not just let Liesel and whoever else finds it have it? We have more money than you could ever need. And if you need a raise, just ask."

It's not about the money. It was never about the money. I wish I could tell him the truth, but it would endanger him and his family. If I told him the truth, he'd murder me for risking his family—something I'd never willingly do.

"I can't tell you."

He narrows his eyes, trying to figure out what I'm not telling him. He won't figure it out. I'm a fantastic liar.

"Are you going to make Liesel pay for what she did?" he asks. He doesn't give away if he wants me to punish her or not. There was once a time when Liesel was his friend too. He knows her more intimately than I do, but Enzo is also a man of honor. He won't let someone hurt his family without consequence, and Siren is his family.

"Yes," I say.

"Good," his voice is strained as he says it like it hurts him, but he knows it has to be done. "Liesel used to be part of this family. She used to get our protection. Not anymore. She chose to leave. She chose to hurt this family. That is the one thing I will never forgive."

I nod, and then I look at him with all the pain of our past. "This is our fault."

"How do you figure?"

"We failed her. We didn't protect her when we should have. Time and time again, we failed to save her from the darkest among us. From your father. From others…"

Enzo turns back to the ocean. It's too painful to know the part we played in making Liesel this way.

"We did fail, but we were kids then. Since then, we have done everything we could to protect her. She made her choices," he finally replies.

"We were never kids, never given the choice to be innocent. We should have protected her. There isn't any excuse that's good enough. Someday, we will pay for that sin." I run my hand through my hair, feeling the salt from the ocean turn my hair into blonde waves. "And I'm not sure we didn't fail again as adults."

"We've had an eye on her this entire time."

"I know, but how did she end up in that twisted game on that boat the first time? How did we miss that?"

"Because she wanted us to. Listen, Liesel isn't innocent anymore. She's a woman who can make her own decisions. You have to let her go. Punish her, get Siren justice, but then let her go."

I can't.

I frown.

"What do you need from us?" Enzo asks.

"One month. I need you to give me one month to get some answers from Liesel, and then I'll end this."

Enzo nods and then pats me on the back. "I'll hold you to that. You have one month, and then I don't want to ever speak of Liesel Dunn again."

He walks back into the house, and I know I won't be able to keep my promise to him. Even if I accomplish everything I need to in one month, I won't be able to give Liesel up. She's in all of my thoughts. She's in my soul, and dare I say it —my heart.

———

I don't waste any time. Enzo gave me a month before he intervenes. That's how long he's willing to put his family, and me, at risk before he makes me give Liesel up.

I stand on the floor of the convention center with a crowd of people who have come to mourn Waylon Brown.

Nolan, his campaign manager, is on stage speaking about how great Waylon was and all the amazing things he would have done as governor.

I resist the urge to roll my eyes. The man was a monster who lent out his soon to be wife to play in a sick game for his own twisted pleasures. The man would have run this state into the ground.

"Let's all have a moment of silence to honor Mr. Brown," Nolan says.

The room goes quiet, and that's when she spots me.

Liesel is wearing a black lace dress sitting in a chair on stage to the right of Nolan. She plays the part of heartbroken fiancée well.

That's because she is heartbroken, even though I'll never

understand why she fell for that old, fucked up man. He had to have brainwashed her.

Our eyes meet through the silence.

This is war, I say with mine.

Good, I'm ready for this to end, hers say.

I smirk as Nolan begins talking again.

I don't focus on him. I focus all of my attention on her, trying to form a plan of how I'm going to kidnap her. I see Maxwell standing to the side of the stage with a large security team. He's not the best, but he has more talent than I originally gave him credit for.

Still, I can easily slip past him to grab her.

How do I want to do this?

Tie her up?

Drug her?

Drag her kicking and screaming?

Threaten her?

So many choices. But this time, when I take her, she won't be leaving my sight, not again.

"Now, I'd like to give Miss Liesel Dunn the stage to say a few brave words. She's the strongest woman I know. And to prove that point, she's decided to continue Mr. Brown's legacy and run for governor on his platform. Miss Dunn, everyone!"

The room breaks out in giant applause.

My gaze stays locked on Liesel's. Her eyes widen until the whites of her eyes are more visible than the hazel. Then her teeth grind in anger as she looks to Nolan, who is applauding her with a smug grin. The bastard forced her hand again.

I smirk. Nolan messed with the wrong woman. She is going to squash him like the bug that he is. He might have political aspirations, but Liesel won't be manhandled.

She stands from her seat and takes her time walking to the mic.

"Thank you, everyone, for your warm welcome. As you know, this moment is the time to mourn Waylon Brown, a man I loved very much. A man who would have done this state proud. A man who was brutally murdered and taken from us too soon. That is the focus of today."

The crowd is silent as she speaks, completely entranced with her. Liesel has always been a good speaker. She knows how to pull anyone to her side.

"While I would love to announce today that I'm running for governor in my late fiancé's place, today isn't the time or place to make such an announcement. Today is about Waylon. I can pledge this to you, though. I will do everything I can to honor Waylon. If that means running, I'll run. If that means dedicating my life to catching his killer and protecting this state, I will. That is the promise I can make to you today."

The crowd applauds her and then starts chanting, "Dunn, Dunn, Dunn."

They are obviously encouraging her to run. Of course, they want a beautiful, intelligent woman who has lost the love of her life to run. She'd easily win.

I doubt she will, though.

Liesel is a strong woman, more than capable of doing the job, but she's cynical. She doesn't believe the world can be changed from a political office. That's one of the many reasons I was surprised to learn she was with Waylon to begin with.

Liesel believes the world is a dark and dangerous place—and the most she can do is survive it. It's the most any of us can do. Anyone who thinks they can change it is just naive, chasing a dream that will never happen.

Liesel introduces a minister to say a prayer, and she once again takes a seat back in her chair.

Everyone bows their head as the minister begins his prayer.

Everyone except Liesel and me. She looks at me like I'm her savior.

I cock my head, not understanding. I must be interpreting her look incorrectly if she thinks I'd be willing to save her after what she did. The only thing stopping me from killing Liesel today is because I need the secrets she has locked away.

She smirks.

Dammit, what is she doing? What don't I know?

I look around the room like maybe she has the place rigged to blow. Liesel wouldn't kill a room full of innocent people, though. *No, if she plans on killing me, it will be personal.*

The event ends, and Liesel and the group on stage wave before heading backstage.

The crowd begins to move toward the exits, but I slowly walk toward where she disappeared, trying to decide how I'm going to kidnap her, once again.

"Sir, if you aren't with the campaign, then you need to exit through the back, please," a man says. He's wearing all black and has white lettering that says security on the front of his shirt. I could easily take him out, but I don't want to cause a scene.

I'll just have to wait outside. I open my mouth to apologize but am interrupted.

"It's okay, Oliver, he's with me," Liesel suddenly says from behind him.

I frown. This is definitely a trap. I don't like this at all.

Oliver nods at me, and I walk past him toward Liesel, who is now walking quickly down the hallway. *What is she doing?*

A few people give their sympathies to Liesel as we pass. She nods politely and thanks them but doesn't introduce me, even though they all stare at me, expecting an introduction.

I don't know what she's going to do if we run into Nolan, Maxwell, or someone who actually has the balls to ask who I am.

Finally, we get to the end of the hallway, and she pushes me into a room before slamming the door shut behind her. She doesn't turn on the lights, but I realize from the cleaning smell that we are in a janitor's closet.

"Kinky. You want to fuck me in a closet at the memorial service for your fiancé. I didn't think you had it in you, but I'll be more than happy to oblige."

"You're disgusting. And if that's what you really think, you're no better. I just killed your best friend, and you're still willing to fuck me? Always thinking with your cock instead of your brain."

I grab her by the neck and shove her hard against the wall, until the beautiful sound of her struggling to breathe hits my ears.

"I didn't come here to fuck you. I came to kidnap you. It's time we end this."

She tries to say something, but she can't.

I release enough for her to speak.

"Good. Take me to your island. Let's finish this," she says.

Of all the ways I imagined kidnapping Liesel, her willingly agreeing to go with me wasn't one of them.

I smirk. "Who said anything about going to my island? My island is too good for you. No, where we are going is much darker, much more dangerous, and only one of us will come back alive."

4

LIESEL

THIS SHOULD BE MY NIGHTMARE—TRAPPED in a dark closet alone with Langston, the man who killed my fiancé. The man who kills as easily as he breathes. With his hand on my throat, I know he can feel my pulse. It should be racing out of fear, but after everything that has happened, I know he's not here to kill me, not yet.

No, my body is screaming for a fucking kiss. For him to steal a kiss from me because if I gave one willingly, it would be a betrayal to Waylon. Now that he's dead, it's almost more important that I don't betray him.

All I can do is lean into Langston and hope he closes the space.

He won't, but that doesn't stop our bodies from edging closer to that ominous cliff. Once we fall over, we won't ever be the same. We won't be able to go back. Perhaps that's why we've never crossed the line. Never done anything other than kiss and play with each other. Never fucked. Never made love. Never been that intimate.

Flashes of him being that intimate with Phoenix are permanently branded across my eyes.

Langston is married to her, but he doesn't love her. That should be enough to ease my pain, but it doesn't.

I will never admit it out loud, but I want Langston all to myself. I want his every breath, every heartbeat, every kiss, every touch, every orgasm. I want it all, as much as I want to kill him for what he's done.

"Where are you taking me, if not the island?" I ask. It's a stupid question I know he won't answer.

"Why? Changed your mind? Not willing to go with me? Because it doesn't matter. If you don't come willingly, I'll enjoy dragging you out of here by your hair."

I don't want to stay here with these horrible people. I don't want to run for governor. I don't want my devastation to be paraded around for political gain. I don't want to deal with Nolan. I don't even want Maxwell following me around anymore. I'm done with this life.

"I'm ready to finish this—whatever this is between us."

"Good." He removes his hands from my neck. And then I can't feel or hear or see him at all. His breath goes silent, and due to how dark the room is, I can't even make out his outline.

He could kill me right here, and I wouldn't even see it coming. *That's how I'd prefer it.* Take me in the night death, without me seeing you hiding in the shadows.

But as the door creaks open, I know that death won't be coming for me today. I won't be gone in the darkness without pain. No, I have to keep suffering over and over. I have to carry my agony with me every day. But that's why I want to end this with Langston. I'm tired of the pain.

We are at the end of the building. It should be easy enough to sneak out. The main problem is the press. If they are waiting for me to exit the building, they'll see us. I don't want to be photographed with Langston; it will draw too many questions from Nolan and Maxwell.

I should tell Langston all of this, but then this is what he does for a living. He knows how to sneak out of any building. He knows how to be invisible.

So I don't say anything as he opens the door and the light shines onto my face once again. It also hits his face, and for a moment, neither of us is sad or mourning our losses. For a moment, the light reflects off the golden specks in his eyes, and he's the happy boy who once protected me.

My heart clenches, missing that boy so damn much. That's the worst part of having Langston in my life—knowing how incredible he can be. Knowing how amazing he must be to Phoenix, how he protects her. Knowing that he's an incredible father to his kids. Langston can be the most protective, caring man, but only to those he chooses worthy. I lost that title a long time ago.

Langston takes my hand roughly in his, but it doesn't stop the sparks from flying. *Why can't my body hate him as much as I do?* That would make this so much easier.

He yanks me hard into the hallway. In the light, his eyes take in my body roughly, and he frowns.

I glare back. I know I look good, so I don't know why he's frowning at my appearance.

"Don't deny that I look fucking hot."

"I won't, but your black dress screams widow. You're too recognizable."

He's right.

"What do you suggest?"

He smirks, and then he shoves me hard into the wall. His hands run up and down the curves of my waist and hips.

"If you were going to touch me, you should have done it in the closet, not here where everyone can see us."

"I'm in charge, not you. And in the closet, I couldn't see you."

In the hallway, we're both illuminated. His eyes covering

my body is torture as he now has his hands planted on my hips, no longer exploring my body.

He's wearing a black leather jacket that he shrugs off and then holds out to me. "Put your arms through."

I turn around as he helps me put the jacket on, my body tingling as I feel his warmth and smell his husky scent in the jacket. He spins me back to face him as he zips the jacket up, hiding most of my dress. Then he grabs the hem of my dress, and I hear a rip.

"What are you doing?" I breathe.

"Making you uncomfortable."

I roll my eyes as I realize he's separating the lace layer from the black material underneath. He rolls the lace of my dress up and ties it around my waist until it's hidden beneath the jacket.

I smile at him.

He frowns, staring at me.

"What's wrong now?"

"Your hair."

I grab at my blonde tendrils. He's not cutting them off; I won't let him.

"Relax," he winks. "Stay here."

He leaves me leaning against the hallway wall for support as he walks back into the closet. A second later, he reappears with a hat.

"How did you know there was a hat in there?" I ask.

"I can see in the dark."

Then he plops the hat on my head, tucking any loose strands of my blonde hair until the hat hides it all.

"Let's go." He yanks me hard into the side of his chest as we walk back down the hallway and out of the convention center, looking like a couple attending. No one pays us any attention. No one knows it's me.

We walk to his parked car down the street. I willingly

climb in, knowing that this could be the last time I step foot in New York City if Langston has his way.

I smile at that. New York wore me down more than I ever want to admit. Langston makes me feel alive, even though he's the one man who could finally end me. But until that time comes, I'm going to enjoy the fleeting feeling.

5

LANGSTON

"Where are we going?" Liesel asks as I start driving away.

"You really think I'm going to answer that?"

She smirks. "No, and honestly, I don't care. As long as it isn't this city."

I frown. *Why does she stay here and build her life here if she hates the city?*

A tear builds in the corner of her eye again. I've never seen Liesel cry before I killed Waylon. Now it seems she doesn't know how to stop.

I still don't understand why she cries for him. *How she could have loved him?*

That and a million other questions are what I plan on finding out.

I drive toward the docks, and Liesel moans.

"Really? Back on the water? Can't you take me anywhere else? A filthy dungeon somewhere swarming with cockroaches and rats?"

I stifle a smile. Liesel always hated the water most of all. I never learned why.

"Why do you hate the water?" I ask.

She looks out the window, and I doubt I'm going to get an answer.

I stop the car and pull into a parking spot next to the dock. We step out of the car, and to my surprise, Liesel speaks.

"The ocean took you away from me," she answers.

My breath catches. She's right; the ocean took me away from her. The ocean led me to Enzo. To earning enormous wealth. To killing.

But I can't be the reason she hates anything. Me getting taken away from her was a blessing for her, not a curse.

My phone buzzes in my pocket.

Phoenix.

I frown. She knows not to call me unless it's an emergency.

I answer. "Siren?" I ask, hoping there's good news. I can't think of the worst.

"No, sorry, it's Rose."

"What happened?"

"I'm taking her to the children's hospital. She's lethargic and in pain. She's asking for you. I told her you have to go on a very important trip, but—"

"I'll meet you there in twenty minutes," I say.

I can hear her relief through the phone. Phoenix is great with the kids, but they've always been closer to me. We share a bond that no matter how much I've disappointed them by having to spend time apart, they still love me. It's why I can't fail them, not in the ways I failed Liesel.

I end the call and look at Liesel, who is staring at me curiously.

"Leaving?" she asks.

I take a heavy breath. I don't want to leave Liesel here. I don't trust she'll be here when I get back, but I have to go. I won't abandon my kids.

"Yes, but you aren't."

She gives me a sad smile. "Where are you tying me up?"

"I'm not."

Her head turns sharply in my direction like she doesn't believe me. There are too many dangerous people after us. She still may not understand that yet, but the treasure that only she and I have all the clues to are infinitely valuable. And she doesn't yet understand that I won't let anyone hurt her, not until I have every secret she holds. She will only die at my hand.

"You're taking me with you?" She raises an eyebrow.

I can't do that either. I can't let her anywhere near my kids.

"No."

"Then what are you going to do with me?"

I pull a gun from my waistband and hold it out to her.

She recoils. She hates guns almost as much as she hates me.

"Take it."

Reluctantly, she takes the gun in her hand. I try to push the last time she held a gun out of my head. *Don't think about Siren.* She's strong. She'll survive.

But I can't help the rage that forms seeing Liesel holding a gun again. I can't believe I'm doing this. I can't believe I'm letting her live.

Not for much longer.

"Don't worry, I won't kill anyone else," Liesel says, trying to get me to explode and end this sooner than I planned.

"Don't push me, Liesel."

"Why? You won't tie me up. You won't kill me. You won't hurt me. You've already taken everything from me. There is nothing left you can do to hurt me."

I run my hand through my hair. "There is nothing left you can do to hurt me either."

"Not Phoenix? Not your kids?"

"I care about Phoenix, but she knows what she signed up for. She knows her role and that it's a dangerous one. Losing Phoenix wouldn't hurt, but then you already deduced that."

"But hurting your kids would hurt you."

I growl, losing my control. I run at her and tackle her to the ground beneath me. "My kids are untouchable, even to you. They can't be hurt. They are more protected than anyone on this planet. You may be a monster, but you won't hurt them."

"How do you know I won't?" She wheezes as I crush her beneath the weight of my body.

"I see through you. You're not the devil you claim to be."

Then I stand up and walk back to the car.

"What am I supposed to do?" Liesel shouts at me as she sits up on her elbows and watches me get in the driver's seat.

"Stay alive until I get back."

"What if I want to run?"

"You don't. But run if you must, I'll enjoy the chase."

Then I slam the door and drive away, knowing that Liesel won't run. She'll be here when I get back. She's tired of running, just like I'm tired of begging for a different, less painful life.

———

"Daddy!" Rose says as I enter her hospital room.

Everything else in my life fades away with one word. My little girl is sitting in a hospital bed that makes her look tiny and small, smiling up at me like she's meeting her favorite Disney character, instead of just her father coming to tuck her in.

I walk into the room where Phoenix is sitting next to her. She looks over at me with a worried expression on her face.

She stands up and touches my shoulder, telling me everything with that touch. Then she walks out of the room, giving us some privacy.

I sit down on the edge of Rose's bed, and then I tuck her blonde curls that match my own behind her ear. I eye the cast covering her arm.

"Fell out of a tree?" I ask with a wicked smile. I should be angry that I had to risk my entire plan to come here and be in the hospital with Rose, all because she has a far too adventurous spirit for a normal seven-year-old.

She blushes. "Mom told me not to, but there was a robin that fell out of the nest. I had to help it back."

I smile, completely in love with my little girl. She's fearless, compassionate, and kind—everything I'm not.

"You know you should listen to your mom when I'm not around."

"I know, but you would want me to save the robin. I knew you would be proud of me, so I had to climb the tree. I had to be brave, just like you always tell me."

I laugh as I pull her into my chest. She's going to continue to be a handful as she grows up. Boys are going to line up for a chance with her, but she's too strong-willed to let any boy into her life.

And I have no doubt she's going to take on the world. I have no idea what she will be when she grows up—a doctor, a veterinarian, a lawyer, an activist, the president. Whatever it is, she's going to make a positive impact on the world and most likely spin it on its head.

I just hope I'm around long enough to see it.

"Dad!" Atlas yells, as he runs inside Rose's hospital room.

I wink at Rose, knowing that Atlas is about to lecture Rose on how careless she was. That's my son, the complete opposite of Rose. While Rose is outgoing, bright, and adventurous, Atlas is introverted, quiet, and serious. He lives life carefully, ensuring that each decision he makes is the right one. He doesn't run head-on into danger like Rose does.

I scoot Rose over as Atlas climbs up onto the bed. I pull him into my other side until I'm hugging both of my kids. If only I could live the rest of my life here like this, holding my two kids—the only people in my world I truly love anymore.

"Rose climbed a tree even though Mom told her not to," Atlas says.

"So I've been told. And what did you do?"

"I tried to catch her when she fell, but I wasn't strong enough."

I notice now that Atlas has some scratches on his arms and his clothes have dirt spots on them.

I smile. My kids are perfect for each other. Rose gets into trouble, while Atlas tries to rescue her. I love them both for exactly who they are. As they grow older, they will continue to look out for one another, getting each other into and out of trouble.

"You did well, Atlas. What do I always tell you?"

"To help Rose. Are you sure I shouldn't have ratted her out and told Mom what Rose was planning?" He gives Rose the evil eye, like she's the reason for all his problems. It's not true. He loves Rose and would do anything for her.

"No, your job is to rescue her when she needs your help."

"I do not need rescuing, ever," Rose pouts.

I bite my lip to hide my smile as I touch the tip of her nose. "I know you don't, but sometimes it's nice to have the help of someone who loves you. You can do great things on your own, Rose, but just imagine how much more you can do with the help of someone who loves you."

She thinks about it, and my words sink in.

I pull them both tightly to my body, hugging them as hard as I can.

"Look out for one another. Love one another. Don't rat

each other out. Don't turn on each other. Protect one another. Can you both promise me that?"

"Yes, Dad," they both say at the same time with bright smiles.

"Good."

"Do you have to leave again?" Atlas asks.

"Not until you two fall asleep. But yes, I have to go. This is for the last time, though. Someday soon, I won't have to go anymore."

"I'm never going to sleep then. That way, you won't ever leave," Rose says.

I kiss her forehead as she yawns. I'm sure the doctors have her on strong pain medication and she'll be asleep very soon.

"I'm going to sleep just like you say. The sooner I go to sleep and you leave, the sooner you'll return," Atlas says.

I kiss his forehead as well.

"Tell us a story, Dad," Rose says, yawning again.

So I do. I tell them the same story I always do about a prince and princess who save the world. It's a true story. Maybe the prince and princess don't actually save the whole world, and maybe technically they aren't royalty in real life, but in my world, they are. And they saved me. Now it's my turn to save them back.

6

LIESEL

I WATCH as Langston drives away, leaving me with nothing but a gun and the clothes on my back.

The only thing I can think of that would make him leave me right now is something happening to Siren. He spoke her name. *Does that mean she's dying? Already dead? Did I finally succeed in killing someone?*

It doesn't matter. He's gone, which means I have nothing to do but wait until he returns. He left me here because he knows I won't run. I'll stay and fight.

I put the gun into the pocket of the leather jacket, and then I walk down the dock to Langston's yacht. This is the safest place to be, at least until Langston returns. Then anywhere Langston is is the least safe place to be.

I climb onto the yacht and then down to the bedrooms. There is a security system that requires facial, handprint, and a code to enter the bedrooms. The bedrooms are designed to be the most secure place on the yacht.

I frown, knowing I'm not going to be able to break in. I'm going to have to sleep on one of the lounge chairs on the upper deck instead of in one of the secure bedrooms.

The laser begins scanning my face, and I put my hand on the scanner. To my surprise, the light turns green. The only thing left is to enter a code.

I enter my old code that used to work, and the door unlocks. Langston never had my codes revoked. He never ended my access. He never stopped hoping that I would return to redeem myself.

He was wrong to wait for my return. He should have known that I would always betray him, just as he's betrayed me.

I walk into the room and climb into the bed, my eyes instantly closing to prevent more tears from escaping.

And then I wait.

———

I don't hear anything, and yet my eyes fly open. They are flooded with tears, as is my pillowcase. I wipe the wetness from my face quickly. So much for sleeping to keep the tears at bay.

I sit up in bed and dig the gun out of the pocket of the leather jacket I'm wearing as I listen carefully for the intruder that I feel in my bones is here.

Stay alive—that's what he said.

I almost want to die just to disobey him.

I hear nothing.

No footsteps, no creak of the floorboard or door, no talking.

It was nothing. I'm just being paranoid.

Goosebumps form on my arms even though I'm plenty warm enough with Langston's jacket wrapped around my arms.

I smile at the reaction, knowing exactly who is on the ship.

The door opens, and I don't even bother to lift the gun to aim.

"That was quick," I say.

"I didn't trust that you could keep yourself alive without me. You have a hankering for getting into trouble whenever possible."

My smile lifts higher. He's right—danger is constantly following me.

Langston steps further into the room. He doesn't turn the light on, but I can make out enough of his outline and the whites of his teeth. He's smiling. He seems happy. Wherever he went made him happy.

"Did you go see Siren? Is she doing better?" I ask, risking changing his mood in an instant for bringing up my latest sin against him.

He growls and walks around the bed before plopping down next to me. He hasn't changed out of his clothes. He stares down at my outfit, recognizing that I haven't changed out of my dress or even taken off my heels.

"They haven't told you how Siren's doing, have they?"

He looks at my face, and I know it's true. They are keeping Siren's status hidden from him so he won't spiral.

"Why didn't you aim the gun at me just now?" he changes the subject.

"Because I knew it was you."

His brows furrow. "How?"

"I always feel when you're near. And only you, Enzo, and Zeke are able to sneak around without making a sound. I knew it was you."

"All the more reason you should have pointed the gun at me."

I shrug. He's right.

"Where were you?" I ask, not expecting him to answer.

He leans his head back against the headboard with a soft

smile. "With my kids. My daughter broke her arm climbing a tree, and I needed to make sure she was okay before we left for a while."

He turns to me. "I promised her it would be the last time I left her. I hate leaving her."

"She sounds like a spirited little girl."

"She is. She's the troublemaker, the adventurer. She has to right the wrongs of the world. My son is more cautious, he's the protector."

My ovaries ache listening to him talk about his children. That's when I realize he isn't being kind by sharing facts about his children with me. He's rubbing it in that he gets to be with his children, while I will never see my child again. It's torture.

I pull the jacket tighter around me like a hug. Even though the jacket belongs to Langston, it still makes me feel comforted.

I feel Langston's eyes on me—he's watching me, trying to read my emotions in the dark. He doesn't have to look at me to feel my torment—it's in the air between us.

He's going to say something else cruel and heartless. Right now, I can't handle it.

"Don't. I know I've hurt you, and you've hurt me, but just don't. I can't right now," I say.

He doesn't speak. I close my eyes to try and block out the pain.

I feel a brush against my hand, and then his fingers wrap around mine until he's holding my hand, comforting me.

"Why are you being nice?" I whisper, my eyes still closed. I'm too afraid if I open them that the tears will spill, and he'll see how weak I am.

"Seeing my kids reminded me of the kids we once were before everything got so damn complicated. Sometimes I wish we could go back to that time and change everything."

I open my eyes. "Me too."

He nods.

"Do you regret setting me up in the game on the yacht, knowing that I killed Waylon?" he asks.

I frown; my answer could reveal too much. It could lead to more questions I'm not ready to answer.

"Do you regret killing Waylon?" I ask, stalling.

His eyes dance left then right across my face, trying to read what I'm not telling him.

"No, I don't regret killing Waylon," he answers.

"I don't regret setting you up, even though I knew the outcome."

He blinks rapidly, like I surprised him.

I guess I did.

"What now?" I ask. We are still holding hands like old friends instead of the enemies we have become.

"We have one month to figure that out."

One month—Langston doesn't have to spell it out for me. We have one month to learn each other's secrets, and then he'll kill me. He'll kill me for whatever sin he thinks I committed against him in the past. And even if he learns that wasn't true, he can't let me live for what I did to Siren.

And I can't let him live for what he did to Waylon.

I yawn. I don't know what time it is, but based on how I feel, I'm guessing the middle of the night.

"Sleep, huntress. Tomorrow we fight. Tonight we sleep."

I sink down onto the pillow, knowing that Langston will sleep next to me. I shouldn't feel safe next to him, and yet it's the safest place I could be. He won't kill me until our month together is up. Until then, he'll protect me from every danger.

I drift to sleep, knowing it's the most peaceful sleep I'll be able to get.

Until a loud bang wakes me up.

7

LANGSTON

I WATCH Liesel close her eyes and fall asleep. She looks so peaceful, so content, but I know that isn't true. Just like all my worries slipping away when I stare at her—it's not reality.

In reality, we are both enemies locked in a battle that will only end in one of our deaths.

I've had a lot of practice watching others sleep over the years. Ever since my kids were born, I've been watching them sleep and ensuring they're still breathing as they snuggle their favorite stuffed animals—Rose, a dragon and Atlas, a traditional teddy bear.

I get the same feelings watching Liesel sleep as I do my children. Liesel feels like my whole world. I have blinders on when it comes to Liesel. I don't see, hear or feel anything but her.

I should sleep. I'm going to need my energy to match her tomorrow. I can't afford for her to outwit me and once again escape or lead me into a trap.

But it's impossible to close my eyes when watching her

sleep soothes my soul in a way that I didn't even realize I need. I reach out and touch her face.

She doesn't stir.

That's when I sink down into the bed and wrap my arms around her body. If I can't keep my eyes on her all night, at least I can hold her.

I don't feel the rage I expect by holding her in my arms. I don't want to destroy her for hurting Siren, or for what she did before. Holding her makes me want to protect her, care for her, even love her.

"Why don't I hate you?" I whisper in her hair. I don't understand—she's done some of the worst things possible against me, and yet, I don't hate her. I'm angry—*yes*. But hate...*I could never hate her.*

But still, I have to ensure that Liesel never commits another sin. I have my kids to worry about. I can't let her anywhere near them. I still can't believe I talked to her about them. I have to protect them from her.

But dammit, do I wish she could meet them. She'd love them. Maybe meeting someone so pure, innocent, and kind would persuade Liesel to my side.

A loud banging noise startles me, and I jump up.

Liesel jumps up as well.

"What was that?" she whispers, wrapping my leather jacket tighter around her. She hasn't taken it off. I want it to be because the jacket comforts her and makes her feel like I'm wrapped around her, protecting her. But she also hasn't changed out of her dress or heels, so I can't read much into her still wearing my jacket.

"Someone's on the boat," I say back.

I find the gun I gave Liesel and hand it to her once again. She takes it weakly, like holding the gun disgusts her.

"Have a problem holding a gun? You didn't seem to have

a problem using one to shoot my best friend," I growl at her, still pissed off.

"I hate this world," she mutters almost to herself as she readjusts how she holds the gun like a pro. She may resist this world. She may act like she doesn't belong. But the way she holds a gun and carries herself, combined with her devious and conniving methods means she belongs as much or more than any of us.

"Stay here. I'll go take care of the danger. The bedrooms are the safest place. I'll put it in emergency lockdown mode. I won't even be able to get back in without you unlocking the door."

I stand up and pull out my own gun. I'm sure it's just another failed attempt to get information about the treasure from Liesel or me. I'll be able to squash whomever this is quickly, but I should move the yacht out to sea to make it harder for us to be attacked.

I consider calling Enzo or Kai to let them know we are being attacked in case I'm wrong and I need their help, but I think better of it. I don't need their help, and I don't want them to worry, not when they should be taking care of Siren and making sure she lives.

I walk to the door before I hear Liesel's strong voice, "Stay."

I turn and look at her.

She's breathing hard, her eyes wild, and she climbs out of bed and runs over to me.

"If this is the safest place to be, then stay. We can wait whomever out."

I smirk. "Worried about my safety?"

She frowns. "No, but I know what it's like to grow up without a father, and I don't want to have to find your kids a new one because you are too proud to call for help when you need it."

Liesel's worried about me. It warms and pisses me off at the same time. She has no right to care about me.

"Liar," I say. She can pretend she's looking out for my kids all she wants, but I know the truth. She only ever looks out for herself.

She blinks like I just slapped her. "Is it so wrong of me to care?"

I touch her cheek. "It's only wrong of you to say you care because of my kids. You're selfish, Liesel. You care about me because you are the one who wants to destroy me."

She shakes her head angrily and steps back. "You're right. I lied. You are my only chance at killing the danger outside this door. I just want you to be smart so that I don't end up stuck in this room without food or water. This gun isn't enough to protect me, and I don't trust you to protect me."

"Don't worry, sweetheart. No matter how many attackers are out there, I'll be able to protect you. I never lose."

And then I kiss her to piss her off.

The kiss starts that way as she tries to push me back with her hand on my chest. Her lips push me away as she bares her teeth, but when her back hits the wall, she moans. She slips up and parts her lips just enough for my tongue to push between her full lips. And her hand grips, instead of pushes, at my shirt.

And then we are kissing, not fighting. It seems the only time we aren't fighting is when our bodies are pressed together. I want more and more and more.

Her moans prove she doesn't want the kiss to stop either.

A loud booming sound jerks us away from each other as we both pant hard.

"Why do I enjoy kissing you so much when all I want to do the rest of the time is end your life?" I say, talking to myself.

"Because I'm an excellent kisser and you're a man. You only think with your cock."

I shake my head. "You're a huntress whose main strategy is to attract her prey with honey and lure them into her trap. I'm no prey. You can't trap me, and we already know you are incapable of killing me."

"I killed Siren."

I grit my teeth and fist my hands. She's trying to goad me. To knock me off-balance so when I leave this room, I won't be on my game. I'll be thinking of killing Liesel instead of focusing on my task.

"Siren isn't dead."

"You don't know that." She smirks.

"I know that if she is, you're a dead woman."

"I'm a dead woman either way."

The way she says it with such a softness and certainty hits me to my bones. She's right, but I didn't expect her to surrender to that truth so soon. I expected more of a fight from her, but maybe killing Waylon did that to her.

"Stay here and use that gun on anyone who tries to get through the door."

Then I open the door and quickly shut it behind me, before keying in a code that puts the whole ship into emergency lockdown. It will keep Liesel safe. I just don't know if she'll ever let me back into that room when the danger has cleared.

I listen carefully, trying to get hints of who and how many attacking are onboard. I don't hear any footsteps, but I do hear a loud banging sound from upstairs, like someone is banging on a door trying to get in.

I crack my neck. After my conversation and kiss with Liesel, I need an excuse to kill someone. It will help get out some of my rage.

I pull out my phone to check the security feed, but no one shows up on any of the cameras.

I frown; whoever is attacking knows how to hack into my security system to make themselves invisible. That's not an easy feat. Not impossible, but not easy.

The assailants are more skilled than I first thought. *But why are they so brazen to make loud noises?* It's almost like they are drawing me out on purpose.

I consider turning back and checking on Liesel, but I don't want her to win. I don't want her to know I have a single feeling for her other than hatred.

Plus, Liesel is completely safe locked in the bedroom.

I head upstairs slowly, even though I want to rush in and start shooting. I want to get my adrenaline pumping. I have to be smart if I'm outnumbered, though.

I inch forward room through room, floor through floor, but I find no one. I reach the top deck, thinking I may have imagined the threat.

I look around the top deck and find no one.

I sigh.

Maybe I'm just being paranoid?

I turn to head back down with my gun at my side when I feel something sharp hit my neck.

I reach back, and I feel a dart in my neck. I yank it out, but whatever drug that was just pushed into my system works quickly. My legs weaken, my heart races, and my eyes spin.

I turn my head, trying to get a look at my attacker, but all I see is the darkness, the moon, the stars. I don't see anyone.

And then I collapse.

8

LIESEL

My head pounds as I open my eyes, and I know things are very, very wrong.

A chill hits my spine despite me still wearing Langston's leather jacket. There must be a hole in the back, letting cool air in.

I blink several times, and then I lift my hand to my head to try and soothe the pounding headache. That's when I feel the weight of chains on my wrists. I look around the room to assess the danger, although I see nothing but darkness.

I'm no longer in the safety of Langston's yacht.

I've been taken.

Did Langston do this? Is this the place he was taking me to get answers out of me?

It must be.

I take a deep inhale, but all I smell is sweat and blood. I try to examine myself, but I don't see any signs of injury, so I don't know where the blood smell is coming from.

There is a quiet drip of water hitting the stone floor. It's the only sound. I don't hear anything or anyone else.

I'm in a prison by myself. I should be thankful I'm no

longer on the yacht, that Langston did what I asked and moved me to a dank dungeon.

I lean my head back against the stone wall to try to keep my head from spinning. I can't remember anything from last night—nothing after Langston left the bedroom to go check on the intruders.

Whatever drugs Langston used are strong.

I move my legs and realize they aren't chained, just my wrists to each other. After my head stops spinning, I force myself to stand and explore my new room. I'm sure there is no weakness. No hole that I can make bigger. No breakable door. No escape. Not this time. But I still have to check.

My hands trail over the wall as I walk around the room. The room is a circle of stone, and my mind creates a medieval tower. I reach up, but I don't touch the ceiling. And after I've walked for a while, I suspect I've walked in a complete circle several times but never found a door.

I frown as I look up. The door must be above me.

"Dammit, Langston! Really? You think you need to lock me up like this to get answers? You coward! Show your face."

A moan.

My eyes dart back to the ground. There is someone in this room with me.

How did I miss him?

I've walked all the way around the room, touching the wall as I go, but I didn't explore the center of the room.

Carefully, I take a step, then another toward the center. I can't see anything, but eventually, my foot hits a soft lump, and I stop, dropping to my hands and feet.

"Hello?" I say as I reach out to touch the person.

He moans once again.

"I'm not going to hurt you. Are you injured?"

The man doesn't answer me, but he slowly sits up. I'm

guessing he's recovering from the same drugs used to knock me out.

I sit patiently by him while he comes to. It's going to take him a moment to process everything.

Finally, I think we're face to face. "Liar. You've already hurt me. I'm sure you'll do it again."

I gasp.

"Langston?"

"Yes, huntress. It's me."

I bite my lip as I stare into his golden eyes. It's dark, but my eyes are slowly adjusting enough to make out the tiny specks of his hair falling over his eyes. It's Langston, and I have no idea what we are both doing locked in this dungeon together. Maybe he locked us both in here so I would have nowhere to run, no safe place to hide for even a moment between him torturing me for truths.

"Please tell me this is your dungeon," I say, realizing I'd prefer that to be the truth than the alternative. I can handle Langston as my enemy. I know him. I know what I'm up against. But an unknown enemy—I don't know how to face that. And if we are really stuck in here together, I don't want to have to fight with Langston by my side.

He winces as he sits fully upright. "This is my dungeon."

"Liar," I breathe.

He curses once again as he tries to move.

"Where are you hurt?" I ask, moving the heavy chains as I reach out to Langston to find the wound.

"Why do you care? If I'm hurt and die, then you win."

I roll my eyes. "Because I'm stuck in a dungeon with no door. My hands are bound together with a heavy metal chain. Unfortunately, you are my only hope of getting out of here alive. So tell me where you are injured so I can make sure you stay alive long enough to kick our attacker's ass."

"I'm not injured. It's just the drugs. Everything hurts when I move."

"Wimp," I say with a smile.

"Yes, I'm a wimp. Sorry, I don't like pain."

Now, I'm smiling.

"Are your arms chained?" I ask.

He lifts them, and I hear them rattle together. "Yes."

"Legs?"

He shifts, and I hear nothing but his feet moving against the stone. "Nope."

"Good." I take a deep breath, trying to think. "What do you remember? Who attacked us? Who is holding us captive?"

There's a beat of silence. "I don't remember anything after I left you alone in the bedroom."

I frown. "Nothing?" *Is he lying to hide facts from me? So he can escape without me?*

"Nothing. Whatever drug we were hit with is strong. We might remember as time goes on. That is, if we live long enough."

Chills hit me again, and I shudder.

"I'll live long enough."

He chuckles. "Not without me, you won't."

"Good thing you want to be the one who kills me then instead of me dying from starvation or hypothermia."

"Good thing."

"I've felt around the whole room. There is no door. I think it must be above us. The entire room and floor is made of stone, so I don't know if you will be able to dig us out or not. There is water dripping on the far side against the wall. That might mean there is a weakness in the structure on that side. What's your plan?"

"To rest."

I frown. "Seriously, what's your plan? We have to work together if we are going to have a chance to escape."

"To. Rest."

"We can't rest. We are trapped in a dungeon. We have to escape. We—"

"Need to rest. You just said there are no doors. There is no way to dig under the walls. We are both weak from being drugged. We need to rest to regain strength. We need to wait and be patient. Whoever is holding us captive will make themselves known soon enough. People are easier to break than walls. Once we have all the facts, then we will be able to escape."

He starts to crawl away from the center of the room until he hits one of the walls, and then he leans against it. His breathing is heavy, and I suspect he is really hurt, he's just not telling me. That's why he suggests we rest.

I move until I'm sitting next to him, leaning against the wall. I try to think of who could be holding us captive.

"Whoever it is, it's about the treasure, isn't it?"

"Most likely."

I close my eyes. "I should have told you the truth. Maybe then you could have gotten it, and everyone would be going after you instead of both of us."

He doesn't answer.

"They are going to torture us for information, aren't they?" I ask.

He doesn't answer again, but I know that's what is going to happen. And I know I'm going to be seen as the weakest. They will torture me, rape me. They'll try to use my pain to break Langston, but it won't work. Even if I told all of my truths, it wouldn't be enough to save me. Langston has the other half of the secret. My secrets alone wouldn't be enough.

Stop thinking like that. For now, I need to do what

Langston said. I need to rest. I need to save my strength so that when the bastard shows his face, I'll be strong enough to face him.

And then I hear Langston speak before I drift back to sleep. "I won't let them torture you. I won't let them hurt you. I'll only let them torture me."

His words should comfort me. But he's told me that before, and he failed me. He didn't protect me. I doubt he can now.

9

LANGSTON

I LEAN against the wall of our dungeon—a tower made of stone with no door, no escape. The room is pitch-black, but I've lived my life in the dark. That I can adjust to. I can see almost as easily now in the dark as I can in the light.

I wish I could say I have a plan to escape, that I know exactly who took us and how to defeat them. But I can't even remember how we were taken. I don't remember anything after kissing Liesel.

I don't know how much danger we are in, but I suspect whoever took us is serious about getting the treasure that only we know the truth about. They took us without a fight, wiped our memory with a drug, and then dropped us in this impossible to escape tower.

Nothing is impossible. I haven't tried to escape. We will be free again. I just need to regain my strength first.

I don't want Liesel to worry, though, so I don't tell her the truth. I don't tell her of the pain in my back that agonizes me with every breath. I don't tell her that I don't have a plan. That I'm not sure I'm strong enough to protect us both.

I just have to protect her. That would be enough.

Flashes of Rose and Atlas pop in my head. *I have to protect us both, for my kids.*

I told Liesel that we should rest, that that was the only thing to do. Really, it was just an excuse to not talk and reveal the extent of my injury to her.

Liesel closes her eyes and, judging by her steady breathing, drifts to sleep.

There is no way I'll be able to sleep with the amount of pain I'm in.

"Are you asleep? I can't sleep," Liesel suddenly says.

I chuckle.

"Can you not tell that I'm not asleep?" I ask.

She bites her lip. "Not all of us have adapted to see in the dark like you."

Good, I like that I can see her, but she can't see me very well. It gives me an advantage. When it comes to her, I'll take every advantage I can get. It was wrong to assume I could just bully her into telling me everything. She's a worthy opponent, playing her own game. Her odds of winning are as strong as mine.

"Let's play our game then since you can't sleep."

"I can't tell you about our secret. Whoever is holding us could be listening. You can't punish me for not telling you the truth when it could endanger our lives."

"No, but you can still tell me a different secret."

She sighs. "Fine, I'll answer a question, but only if you answer one of mine as well."

"That's not how this works."

She folds her arms. "Then kill me. We are trapped in a dungeon for who knows how long. There is nothing worse you could punish me with. You aren't going to kill me until we escape and you get all your answers out of me, so your threats won't work here."

She's right. "You answer one of my questions; then I'll answer one of yours."

"With the truth?" she asks.

"That's up to you to figure out."

She smiles knowingly. "Fine. What's your question?"

I have a million, but one pulls at me more than any other. One I still don't understand.

"Did you love Waylon?"

She stills, not expecting that question. Her eyes glaze over as memories flood her head. She's no longer in this room with me; she's lost to her thoughts.

I give her time to think about Waylon, about how she's going to answer me.

I study her every feature looking for clues as to how she feels about the man. She was so distraught that I killed him that she tried to take one of the most important people in my world from me. Her actions speak louder than any words, and yet, I still feel like I'm missing something. I didn't think Liesel was capable of loving another man, loving anyone.

"Love is weakness. I have no use for love," Liesel finally speaks, not looking at me, just staring out into the darkness.

"That doesn't answer my question."

"I'll answer you honestly because I have a question I want you to answer with the truth." Her eyes flick to me. I know she can't see anything but an outline of my body when she looks at me, but that doesn't stop me from feeling like she can see everything I'm thinking.

"I tried my entire life to not fall for a man. I tried to keep love out of the equation. I tried...and failed."

Tears water her eyes, but it's nothing compared to how my heart aches. She drives me mad, and yet there is nothing in this world I want more than to hear she has feelings for me. To hear her admit she has feelings for another man is going to break me.

"I changed my mind. I don't want to hear your answer," I say, admitting my own weakness to her.

"I loved Waylon." She plunges the knife into my heart.

She loved him, and I took him from her.

"You loved him even though he sold your body for money? Even though he made you suck other men's cocks to set a trap for me? Even though he wasn't strong enough to protect you, you loved him?"

"Yes, I loved him. I'll always love him."

"I didn't think you were capable of love, huntress."

"I didn't think you were either, killer."

"And yet, we both fell in love."

"Do you love Phoenix?"

"Is that your question?"

"No," she quickly replies.

I don't answer her, but she already knows I don't love Phoenix. I've never felt romantic love. I love my kids. I love Siren as my soulmate. I love Enzo, Kai, Zeke, and even Liesel as friends, but I've never been in love, never fallen for another human.

"How did you fall for him? What was it about him that made you surrender to your feelings?"

"It wasn't a choice. It just happened. I tried to fight it, but I couldn't. It was everything—his charm, his kindness, his loyalty. The more I spent time with him, the more I fell. I didn't even realize I was falling until it was too late. I never said the words to him. I never told him I loved him. I don't think I realized how much I loved him until he was gone."

I shake my head. "Ironic then that me killing him revealed your true feelings for him."

She scrunches her nose, narrowing her eyes, as she tries to understand what I'm not saying.

"You would have let him live if it meant that I never revealed how much I loved him?"

"No, I would have still killed him." I had to. He would've ruined her.

She sighs defeatedly and then leans her head against the stone.

"Your turn," I say.

"What?"

"Your turn to ask a question."

"Oh."

She hesitates for a moment, and I suspect she's going to ask about my feelings. Is there anyone I love outside of Siren and the kids? I wouldn't know how to answer that because I don't understand my feelings toward Liesel.

I implore her to ask any question other than that one. I don't want to lie to her anymore. If I lie, she'll lie in return. And then I'll never get what I want.

My teeth grind together as the pain consumes me again. Any time I'm not completely focused on Liesel, the pain returns.

I turn my head and look at Liesel, letting all my stray thoughts I almost never let myself think into my head.

I let Liesel's beauty strike me; I let myself admire every feature that I usually try to ignore. Her bright eyes and red lips are my favorite, but I miss her smile, her laugh. And I have no idea how to make her do either of those things anymore.

I'm the man who makes her cry for the first time in years. I'm the monster who stole the love of her life away from her. I'm the man she will never forgive even though I know I did the right thing for her. Waylon Brown was a bigger monster than me. He would have destroyed her.

You're going to destroy her, too.

"Stop looking at me like that," Liesel says.

I frown, not believing she can see me well enough to know the thoughts in my head.

Still, I drag my eyes away from her face.

"Where are you hurt?" she asks.

"What?"

"My question that you have to answer honestly. Where are you hurt?"

My eyes drag back to her, and I realize her lie. She can see in the dark as well as I can. Or at least, better than she let on.

I shake my head, annoyed with her. "You little liar."

She smiles, smugly. "I know you too well, killer. You can't hide your winces, your tense pained smile, or..." She touches the stone near my back and then lifts her hand up to my face. "...the blood that you are leaking."

She raises her eyebrows at me.

I take her hand covered in my blood and bring it to my lips. I wait for her to fight me, to try and wiggle her hand out of my grasp.

She doesn't move.

I put her fingers in my mouth, and I suck—tasting the iron of my own blood, but more importantly, getting to touch her.

She closes her eyes, and I can see how much I'm turning her on and how hard she's trying not to let her body be excited.

I pull her fingers out of my mouth as I suck them clean. "I should have known that I can't hide anything from my huntress."

She pulls her hand back into her lap. "Turn around," she orders with hooded eyes.

I do as she asks until my back is facing her and I'm sitting cross-legged.

"Let me know if anything hurts," she says, and then she places her hands on my shoulders.

I suck in a breath, not from pain but from agony. My body aches with needing more of her. Needing her touch, her kisses, her everything.

My eyes squeeze shut, and my body trembles as she lifts the hem of my shirt up so she can touch my skin directly.

"Sorry, did I hurt you?"

I shake my head, unable to form coherent words.

She hesitates, like she doesn't believe me. But then her hands are on my bare skin. Gently, feeling over my back, looking for the wound.

I hiss when she hits a spot about halfway up the left side of my body.

"I think I found it."

I nod, knowing she did.

She leans close to my back until I can feel her hot breath on my back, sending fiery goosebumps up my spine. My body is as conflicted as my heart and mind are. I'm not sure if I welcome Liesel's touch or if I want to run away from her as fast as I can.

"It doesn't look like a bullet hole, but I should feel inside and make sure there isn't a bullet fragment inside."

I nod again. This woman has made me mute.

"Tell me about your kids."

"Why?"

"Just do it." I know she's rolling her eyes at me in annoyance even though I can't see her.

"Rose is a free-spirit, always getting into trouble. I remember one time she jumped out of one of my boats into the ocean because she saw a bird dive into the water, and she thought it needed rescuing. She didn't realize that that is how some birds fish."

Liesel laughs. "What happened next?"

"Rose knows how to swim, but she was only six years old, and the waves were strong. I stopped the boat and was about to jump in after her, but before I could Atlas jumped into the ocean too, trying to save her." Now I'm laughing. "Him jumping in only made it more difficult for me to save them both. He was wrapped around Rose, trying to save her, but it was more like the weight of his body wrapped around her neck was drowning her. Neither of them was in any real danger; I got them out seconds after they jumped in. But we had to have a long talk about wearing life jackets and not jumping into the ocean without an adult's permission, no matter the reason."

"You know you and I used to swim in the ocean alone when we were their age."

"You and I did a lot of stupid, dangerous things when we were kids. It doesn't mean my kids get to do the same thing."

"You're a good father."

I don't know why her words make me smile. Apparently, I need her approval more than I realized.

"I didn't find a bullet."

"What?"

She pulls my shirt down. "I didn't find a bullet, but we should tie your shirt around it to prevent any more blood from escaping and try to protect the wound a little."

I realize now that she got me talking about my kids to distract me.

"Thank you." I pull my shirt off and hand it to her.

She takes it and begins wrapping it around my body before tying it off.

"Here," she says, shrugging my leather jacket off. "This will keep you warm."

I turn and stop her from removing the jacket. "Keep it."

"But you need it more."

"No, I'll let you know if I need it. Keep it for now." I like seeing my jacket on her. I like that at least part of me can protect her and keep her warm.

I don't know who is holding us captive. I don't know what their intentions are. But I do know that with me injured, and us both held in this stone tower, an escape is going to be difficult. We are going to have to hope that Enzo and Kai noticed our kidnapping and are on their way. I'm not sure I can get us out of this situation in one piece.

I've vowed to protect Liesel so many times. And each time, I've failed. I doubt this time will be any different. All I can do for now is to try to reassure Liesel that I can protect us, even when I can't.

The only people in this world I can absolutely protect are my children. These monsters can hurt me and Liesel, unfortunately, but they will not hurt Rose or Atlas.

10

LIESEL

LANGSTON IS TRYING to be strong for me. He's trying to protect me, but he can't—no one can.

And he doesn't realize that I don't want to be protected, not anymore. There is only one thing in this world I care about, and that person is gone.

"We should sleep," I say.

Langston nods. "Come here." He holds out his arm, wanting me to snuggle against his chest.

"I can't. I don't want to hurt you." *I don't want to hurt me.* I don't want to get attached to him again like I did when we were kids.

I start to lie down on the ground next to him, when he reaches his hand out and yanks me to him.

"You can't hurt me, huntress. Not any more than you already have." His words strike me like he intended. But I'm not sorry for hurting Siren, just as he's not sorry for hurting Waylon.

"And you can't hurt me anymore. But if we both hate each other, why hold me all night?"

He holds me tighter until my head is forced onto his bare chest. I bite my lip, holding my breath and hoping he doesn't push me off of him because this is nice. It's comforting even though I know he can't, and won't, protect me.

"The same reason that you helped with my back."

"And what reason is that?"

"Sleep, Liesel."

He never answers, and I don't ask any more questions. For now, we are on the same side against a common enemy. We are going to have to work together to get out of here alive.

————

Light shines in my face, and I open my eyes. I'm still lying on Langston's bare chest; my hand is resting on his steel abs.

I let my eyes raise, but I can't see Langston's face. I can't tell if he's awake or still asleep. His breathing is slow and steady, so I assume he's still asleep.

That means I can explore his body without him knowing. My fingertips glide over his abs, feeling every ripple, every hard protrusion. My hand skips over his shirt tied around his torso. It's not completely soaked with blood, so the wound at his back must be healing. Then my hands stroke the thick muscle on his upper chest.

I try not to focus on how good he feels beneath my hand. He's just a man who has a lot of muscle that encases a steel heart—a heart that only softens for his wife and kids. It will never soften for me.

My hand moves up his neck to his face before I realize that his eyes are open and he's staring at my hand.

"What are you doing?" he asks.

I freeze, but that only means that my hand is lying awkwardly like I'm stroking his cheek.

"Checking to make sure you don't have any other wounds you're hiding."

He smirks and shakes his head slowly. "In the light of day, you can easily see that I don't have any wounds on my chest and face. But if you'd like to see if my cock has any wounds I missed..." he winks at me.

I roll my eyes and remove my hand from his face as I sit up.

"Phoenix is a lucky woman," I say sarcastically.

"She is—don't pretend to be offended that I would touch another woman while I'm married to Phoenix. You had a similar relationship with Waylon. Not every marriage is about passionate love."

"Why are you married to Phoenix?"

"It's not time for questions yet. You can ask me tonight in exchange for answering one of my own questions. Right now, we should eat."

"Eat? Unless we are planning on eating each other's limbs, we don't have anything to eat."

"You're such the observant one." Langston nods in a direction across the room.

I turn and see a tray of food is sitting on the ground opposite us.

"How and when did that get in here?" I ask.

He shrugs. "We were both asleep." He moves to get up, but I put a hand on his chest. He needs to save any strength he has to help us get out here.

I walk over and pick up the tray and then place it in front of us.

We both stare at the food—two sandwiches, two bananas, and two cookies, along with two bottles of water.

"Do you think it's poisoned?" I ask, hesitantly. My mouth is watering at the sight, and my stomach growls softly. It's been over twenty-four hours since I last ate. I'm hungry, but not so hungry that I would risk my life yet for food. But Langston could really use the food for strength.

"There's only one way to find out." Langston grabs one of the sandwiches and takes a big bite.

I stare wide-eyed before I grab my own sandwich and bite into it. It's peanut butter and jelly, I realize as I chew.

Langston shakes his head at me. "You were supposed to wait and see if I dropped dead."

"I don't want to be left in this dungeon alone."

Langston's face softens at my words. "Eat. We are going to need our strength."

We both eat in silence. We finish every bite, and every moment that passes reassures us further that the food wasn't poisoned.

"What are you thinking about?" Langston asks.

"How we could escape."

"Do you have a plan?"

I stare up, seeing a high window on the wall. "Maybe, but I'm not sure your wound is healed enough to try it. And I'm not sure I'm strong enough either."

Langston stares up at the window. "Let's try it."

We both stand up, and I remove the leather jacket so that I'm a little more mobile. I feel Langston's heated stare on me in my black dress. The jacket covered most of my curves, but now they are on full display and Langston is appreciating every inch of my body beneath the black fabric.

I clear my throat, and Langston's eyes meet mine. "Do you want to give me a boost, or do you want me to give you one?"

"Let's try you first; you were always a better climber than me," he replies.

I smile, but then I realize it will be hard to climb in this dress. I kick off my heels and hike up my dress until my black panties are exposed. I tie the dress just above my hips to give my legs more mobility.

"If you keep staring at me like that, I'm going to poke your eyes out. I'm not yours to stare at."

Langston walks over to me; brushing the hair off my neck until he thumbs my pulse. "Aren't you? You've always been mine, huntress. That's one of the reasons I'm so angry at you. You've always been mine, and yet you run off with other men."

I narrow my eyes as I glare at him. "Just like you ran off with other women. You got married. You had two kids. You don't get to be mad at me for falling for a man who isn't you. Not when you abandoned me. Not when you couldn't protect me. I've never been yours, killer."

He breathes on my neck, before he turns me around to face him with his hands on my hips. "That's where you're wrong, huntress. You've always been mine, since we were kids. But being mine doesn't mean that I'm going to gives you roses and pamper you. It doesn't mean I'm going to marry you and choose you over all others. Being mine means you are mine to do what I want with. To kiss, to fuck, to kill. Your life is in my hands—even here. Remember that."

"There was once a time when I might have been yours. But then you betrayed me; you failed me. From that moment on, I learned that I belong to no one, and no one belongs to me. I'm not property—I belong to no one. Not even you." I step back until Langston is no longer touching me. He has a scowl on his face, but he doesn't say anything else.

He walks to the wall, assessing the best strategy. "Climb on my back and then up onto my shoulders. I'll boost you as high as I can, and then you can try to climb from there."

I nod, agreeing with his strategy.

Langston leans down so I can climb on his back. I spot

his wound that has bled through the T-shirt tied around his back.

I sigh and climb onto his back, careful to avoid hitting his wound. Although, he deserves for me to drive a knife into his wound, deep into the muscle until he can no longer walk.

Langston stands as I wrap my arms around his neck.

"Now, try to climb up to my shoulders."

I try to ignore how it feels to have his torso between my legs as I scramble up onto his shoulders until my legs are wrapped around his neck.

"Good, now can you stand up?"

I roll my eyes. "Of course, I can stand up. Are you strong enough to hold me up is the question."

He growls as I grab onto his head and press one foot into his shoulder. With a thrust of other my other foot, I'm flung up onto his shoulders.

I don't have to look down to know he has a smug expression on his face. I should know better than to doubt his strength. His body may be lean and injured, but he has an unlimited amount of strength when he wants it.

Standing on Langston's shoulders, looking up toward the window didn't give me much of a boost. I'm still a good twenty or thirty feet from the window. Even if I make it to the window, I'm not sure how I'll be able to get Langston out. A rope maybe, but if I can't find a rope, my only choice will be to run and try to get help. While Langston will be left here...

"On the count of three, I'm going to push you up until you can reach the rock jutting out. Think you can grab onto it?"

"Yes," I breathe, not wanting to think about how painful it would be if I fell and didn't grab onto the ledge.

"One, two, three."

Langston catapults me up, and I feel like I'm flying

through the air as I reach up to the small piece of outreaching stone. When my hand touches the stone, I grip on hard and dig my feet into tiny grooves below.

My entire body is pressed against the cool stone, which helps to keep me from sweating and losing my grip.

"Nice job," Langston says with relief in his voice.

I tilt my head to look at him.

"Don't look down," he says.

I smile. "Why? You're the one who's afraid of heights, not me."

"Just focus. I'll help tell you where your next handhold and foothold is." His voice is stern and commanding, which only makes me smile brighter.

I look up, but all I see is an endless amount of stone bricks. There are no other large pieces of stone sticking out like this one. My handholds are going to get smaller and smaller going up.

I grit my teeth together, determined to reach the window. I'll find a way to get Langston out. I won't leave the stubborn asshole. I won't let anyone else hurt him; that's my job.

I start to reach up with my right hand to find the next handhold.

"A little to your left," Langston says.

I move my hand to the left.

"There."

I feel the hole. It's not much to hold onto. I lift my other hand.

"A little higher," I hear Langston's calm voice.

I move an inch higher until I find a crevice. I take a deep breath, and then I let go of the ledge and push myself up to my new handholds.

"Good job. Take a deep breath and then move again. You got this, Liesel."

I laugh. "Did you turn into a cheerleader?"

"The kids play all sorts of sports and dance recitals. It's just my dad cheerleader in me coming out," he chuckles.

God, what I wouldn't do to see Langston on the sidelines of his kids' soccer game, cheering them on like a regular dad. My heart melts.

As I cling to the side of the tower fifteen feet up in the air, I realize that I won't kill Langston. I have to protect him even though he's failed to protect me. I won't let any more kids grow up fatherless. His kids need him. And I need to get us out of here so he can go protect them.

I take a deep breath, more determined to reach the window.

I reach up faster this time than the last.

"Take your time; there's no rush."

I purse my lips and breathe out as I reach another hand-hold and then foothold. I hoist myself up.

I can hear Langston let out an audible breath when I pull myself up now at least twenty feet up in the air, but a good five to ten feet away from the top.

I can do this. I can reach the top.

I start to reach up, trying to find a handhold big enough that I can cling to. After testing a couple of spots, I can't find one big enough to get a grip.

"Try an inch higher if you can."

I reach higher, but the one Langston suggested is just as small as the rest.

"Climb back down and we can think of a new plan. Those holds are too small."

I hear Langston's voice, but I refuse to believe it. There isn't another way out. This is the only way. And we have to get out, for Langston's kids' sakes.

I refuse to give up so quickly. I reach up, take a deep breath, and pull myself up.

Somehow, I'm still holding onto the wall, but as I reach up again, I can cling onto the wall no longer. I'm going to fall.

No, I'm falling.

My nails try to dig into the wall as my body drops down, but it's no use. For a second before I hit the ground, it's freeing. *Maybe this is how I'll die, trying to save a man whom I care about more than I'll ever admit out loud?* I'll die fast and swift. That's too much to hope for. More than likely, I'll break a leg, an arm, a rib.

I close my eyes, relenting myself to my fate.

Suddenly I hit a soft lump instead of the stone floor.

"Oof," Langston says as I land on top of him.

I blink rapidly, not believing I'm still alive, let alone uninjured after that fall.

Then I look down at Langston beneath me. "Langston!" I shout as I roll off of him.

His eyes are closed as he lies on his back. I hold my hand over his chest. It rises and falls—he's still breathing.

"Langston Pearce, wake up right now!" I yell at him; my voice erratic and terrified.

I try to check him over without moving him, but I suspect he has a head injury, and I need to stop any bleeding on the back of his head.

I yank my dress off and slither it under his head to stop any bleeding and provide some support.

"Langston, wake up!"

An eye opens, and he moans.

"Shh, don't move." I sit back on my heels, a little more relaxed now that I know he's conscious.

He grins at me so large that I can see a dimple. "I'm fine, huntress."

He moves to sit up, but his eyes roll, obviously dizzy.

I grab onto his arm, slowing his movement. "Easy. You hit your head."

I reach back and grab my dress, pressing it to the back of his head where I see the blood coming from. I shake my head at him. "You buffoon, you should have let me hit the ground instead of trying to catch me. You could have been seriously hurt."

"If I'd let you hit the ground, you would have been seriously hurt."

"I don't understand you. You say I deserve to die for what I've done, and yet, you refuse to let me die when I should."

"You can't die until I get all of your secrets." That's what his mouth says, but his body says, *I can't let you die until I have you. Until you're screaming my name. Until I've claimed you as mine in every way.*

"Well, you can't die until we find a way out of here."

He smiles.

"How are you feeling?"

"I have a headache, but otherwise, I'm fine."

I scowl as I crawl to his back to take a look at his head wound. I remove the dress. "There's blood, but it doesn't look too deep."

I tie the dress around his head to apply pressure, but I think he's going to be fine.

"Here," Langston says, holding out the jacket to me. It's only then I realize I'm only wearing a bra and panties.

"Thanks," I say, taking the jacket back and putting it back on before zipping it up. I'm a little reluctant to put it on as I'm enjoying Langston's gaze, but he needs to focus on healing, not eye-fucking my body.

I sigh. "Now what? I don't see any other way out other than that window."

We both lean our heads against the wall. "Now, we wait for whoever is holding us to show themselves and their intentions. Then we try to find their weakness and exploit it."

I nod. I know it's our only option, but it doesn't sound like a good option. "Who do you think is holding us?"

Langston shrugs. "Someone after the treasure."

The window at the top opens, and a gun is aimed down at us.

"Liesel, get behind me," Langston says as we both scramble to our feet.

"No, we fight this together." If anything, I plan on jumping in front of him to take a bullet. He needs to stay alive more than I do.

"Liesel," Langston warns. His voice says he's going to kill me if I don't do exactly as he says, but that warning has never stopped me before.

A bullet rains down on us—we both move. We should be diving out of the way, trying to duck for cover, but that's not how we move. We both lunge toward each other, trying to take the bullet to save the other.

That's the problem with Langston and me—we can pretend we hate each other, that we are enemies all we want, but in reality, we care about each other more than we'll ever say. Our actions speak louder than any words.

We both fall to the ground.

I look down at my torso. I haven't been hit.

"Langston," I whisper. He's taken all the injuries, while I've endured none. If he got shot, I'm not sure he'll have enough blood or strength to make it out of this cell.

I roll him over onto his back so I can examine him. His eyes are closed, but he's breathing. My hands race over his body, looking for the injury. I spot it in his neck. It's not a bullet—it's a dart.

I glance back up at the window just as another dart is shot—this time at me. I squeeze Langston's hand as the dart hits my arm. My eyes grow heavy quickly, and my breathing slows.

We're about to meet our captors, but I can't think straight. All I can focus on is holding Langston's hand as I collapse on top of him.

11

LANGSTON

My head feels like I've been hit with a thousand bricks when I come to. I sit up slowly, expecting to no longer be in the tower, but as I look around, I'm still in the same dungeon. The sun is just starting to set and cast a shadow on the ground.

"Liesel," I breathe, but I already sense the loss. She isn't here. She's been taken out of this room while I was unconscious.

I scramble to my feet, and my body realizes instantly it's a mistake. I shake, my stomach writhes, and I almost vomit. But I push past all of that, just like I push past the pain in the back of my head and back. My body is slowly falling apart, but it's nothing compared to how my heart feels.

I failed Liesel, again.

I failed.

I've wanted nothing more than to protect her. She owes me an explanation, but she doesn't get to die at another person's hand.

"Liesel!" I shout, like she's somehow going to reappear out of thin air. Rage floods my veins as I spin around the room, trying to come up with something, anything, to save her from the hell I'm sure she's in.

I don't know who has taken us, but it doesn't take much to guess that she's currently being tortured by our captors while I sit down here useless.

There are only three options for trying to escape from this tower.

Climb out.

Dig out.

Or break out.

Climbing seems like the most likely option, but after watching Liesel attempt it yesterday, I don't think I'll make it very far.

Still, I move to the wall. I put my hands into the stone bricks and begin to hoist myself up. The climb starts easy enough, but quickly my fingers struggle to fit into the holds. No matter how determined I am to reach Liesel, I can't climb higher.

As hard as it is, I let go and land on my feet back on the ground.

I don't waste time. I move around the room where the wall meets the floor and look for any weaknesses that I could use to start digging my way out.

The best I can find is a small crack in the corner of one of the stones. Liesel's high-heeled shoes are lying on the floor. I grab them and use the heel to start digging. But after twenty minutes, I've barely made a dent.

I don't know what's happening out there, but I won't make it in time to save her from the worst of it, whatever she faces.

I stand up, considering my last option of breaking through a wall. I slam my body as hard as I can against one of the walls. I know it won't help, but it feels good to hit something, to feel something.

I yell at the top of my lungs as I slam my body again. And then tears burn my eyes as I collapse in a pile of worthlessness.

It's no wonder Liesel and I drifted apart over the years. I've failed so many times to protect her, to help her, to save her. This time is no different.

"Take me instead! I know more about the treasure than Liesel. Take me!" I shout up, hoping someone is listening.

I can't think beyond making sure Liesel is safe. I don't care what happens to me, but I can't stay down here, losing my mind while Liesel is being hurt upstairs.

My mind is going wild with all the ways Liesel could be tortured as I collapse back onto the floor, grabbing Liesel's shoe and resuming my futile digging. It may be useless, but it's the only thing that allows me any progress in getting to her.

Images of her beaten, whipped, tied-up, tortured—they all flicker through my brain. Of her being raped, again.

Jesus, why did I think Liesel deserved death? She's already died a thousand times, and somehow she's survived. I can't blame her for her sins after everything she's been through.

If she survives, I should tell her the truth. I should tell her how I feel. I should…

I hear a creak of the window, and I look up.

"Let her go! Take me instead," I shout as I stand.

The dark shadow peering down from the window doesn't speak.

"Please," I beg.

The shadow turns, and then he's lowering something into the tower.

"Liesel," I breathe when I see her limp body being lowered to me.

I can't tell if she's injured or hurt; I can't even tell if she's alive. All I know is she's returning to me.

As soon as her body is low enough for me to reach her, I grab the rope and cradle her in my arms.

"Huntress, it's me. Wake up, baby."

She doesn't stir, but I can feel her warmth, her breathing, her heartbeat. She's alive, and from a quick glance, I don't see any major, life-threatening injuries. That doesn't mean she's not hurt, though.

I lower her to the ground and remove the rope from her body as I hover over her.

I should be focused on getting answers from the dark shadow above me. I should focus on figuring out who he is, but all I can do is focus on Liesel.

I grab her hand and hold it tightly. "I'm here, now. You're safe. I'm here."

I try to bring her comfort, but I don't even know if she can feel or hear me.

She's still wearing my leather jacket and her black panties, which brings me some relief. But there are plenty of things that could have happened invisible to the naked eye. Some of the most effective torture twists your mind more than your body.

I stroke her face as I hold her hand. I want her to wake up, to talk to me and tell me she's going to be okay. But I suspect after what she went through, sleeping is kinder than waking her up. If she's asleep, she doesn't have to face the pain yet.

Plus, I need to make sure there are no visible injuries on her body that I should take care of first. I start with her head and her legs. I don't see any marks, cuts, or bruises. I exhale to find no bruising between her legs. I unzip her jacket and gasp.

Black and blue bruises cover her entire torso.

My hands fist, the vein on my forehead pops, and my nostrils flare. I'm going to kill whoever did this to her.

I study the rest of her body carefully as to not injure her further. I don't find any cuts or lacerations—no external blood. But from the placement of her bruising—she's broken several ribs. It's going to be hard to move, to even breathe for a while. And there could be internal damage she'll never recover from.

What I wouldn't give for some ice or frozen peas right now. For some painkillers, anything that could help her. Instead, all I can do is watch over her. All I can do is watch and wait for her to wake up and hope the pain she feels is less than what I fear.

I pull her head into my lap, hold her hand, and watch her sleep. I pray that when she wakes up, she's not irreversibly broken.

———

Liesel's eyes flicker open, and my heart stops. I hold my breath, not sure what she's going to say, how much pain she's going to be in, or how my heart is going to break for once again failing her.

"I'm here, huntress. I'm here. I've got you."

Her head is still lying in my arms, and I'm still holding her hand. I doubt I, a monster in her eyes, am providing her any comfort. But I don't let go of her hand—I won't unless she does.

"Killer? What happened?"

I look at her with concern. I'm sure the drugs they shot her with made her memories fuzzy, but it won't last long. My memories came back quickly after I awoke; hers will too.

"How are you feeling?"

She blinks, trying to push through the fog. "My head is spinning, but otherwise, I don't feel too bad."

"Do you want to try sitting up?"

Her eyes look up at me. "Only if you'll hold me. I'm not sure I'm strong enough to sit up on my own."

I smile at her. There is no way in the world I'm letting go of her unless she begs me to. And even then, it would take all of my willpower.

"I won't let you go, not until you tell me to."

She nods.

Then I lift her gently until she's sitting up, leaning her back against my chest.

She hisses as she moves.

"Your ribs?" I ask.

She nods.

"It feels like I'm being stabbed with a hundred knives while being sat on by a thousand-pound elephant."

"I'm pretty sure you have several broken ribs."

She looks down at the jacket that I zipped back over her body. She finds the zipper and slowly opens it. Then she gasps.

I look over her body and notice the bruising looks worse than when I first examined her. This is because of me. Every terrible thing that has happened to her is because of me.

"I'm sorry," I whisper.

"You have nothing to be sorry for. You weren't the one who did this."

"Do you know who did this?"

"No."

"Then how do you know I didn't do this to you?"

She smiles. "Because you would never hurt me."

"I've hurt you dozens of times. I've threatened to kill you. I would definitely hurt you."

"Not like this."

"Tell me what you remember," I say. I need to know what happened. I need to know every detail so we can put the pieces together and hopefully find a way out of this.

She takes a deep breath, and I can sense how much it hurts her to just breathe. Although, she tries her best to hide her pain. She tries to hide her moan, her wince, her agony.

"Don't hide how you feel from me. Please, I need to know so I can help you."

"Help me move so I can look at you."

I help her adjust in my lap so that I'm still holding her, but I can see her face. She doesn't hide her moan this time. She lets it out.

It breaks me.

She notices my reaction, but we don't speak about it. I'm not supposed to feel anything for her. I'm not supposed to care. And I can't admit that I do, ever.

"What do you remember, huntress?"

I stroke her face, and she shivers, which makes her cough in pain.

I withdraw my hand from her face, resisting the urge to comfort her in case it might bring her more pain. But I keep holding her hand. I still haven't let it go from the moment she was lowered back into our dungeon.

"I remember the gun being aimed down at us. I remember us both diving toward each other. I remember you being hit in the neck." She reaches up and touches my neck, examining me for any injury.

"I'm fine. I was knocked unconscious while you were taken, but I awoke here and alone, with no injuries."

Her hand runs down my neck to my arm, where I have some bruising, and she looks at me with an accusatory stare.

"I, um, I did everything I could to get to you. I tried climbing, digging, and even ramming myself into the wall to see if it would break."

Her eyebrows drop, and her eyes narrow suspiciously. "You shouldn't hurt yourself trying to save me."

I shake my head. She still doesn't understand that I would do anything to save her, even from myself.

"Tell me what else you remember."

"I remember holding you as you fell unconscious, and then I remember the dart hitting me in my arm."

I nod. "And then?"

She sits for a moment, staring off into space. "And then, nothing but black, coldness."

"What about after you were lifted up?"

She shakes her head. "All I remember is darkness."

"You don't remember how you got these bruises?"

She thinks for a moment, like she should be able to remember, but from her blank expression, she doesn't seem to have her memories yet.

"You don't remember being questioned?"

She shakes her head.

"You don't remember your attacker's face?"

She shakes her head, and then her hand brushes over the bruises on her body. It's one thing to be attacked and tortured. To be able to fight back. To try and defend yourself. To remember and plot your revenge. It's another thing entirely to have your memory of that event taken from you.

I pull her tighter to me, trying my best not to hurt her as I hold her. Liesel was tortured and doesn't remember. That kills me. It kills me that she went through something and didn't even gain the benefit of learning who her attacker was.

And yet, I can't help but think she could be lying to me. She might remember what happened to her, but it was so horrible she can't bear to tell me. By lying, she's trying to protect me.

Oh, my huntress, stop trying to protect me. We can't protect each other. All we can do now is survive together.

LIESEL

I DON'T REMEMBER what happened after I was darted. According to Langston, I was taken out of the cell while Langston remained. When I awoke in the dungeon, I have bruising all over my torso like I was beaten for information, of which I have no recollection. I should examine how the rest of my body feels, but I'm too afraid to find that I've been violated in other ways without remembering.

Instead, I focus on how good it feels to be held in Langston's arms. He's been holding my hand since I awoke and hasn't let it go. For now, I hope he never does.

We are two broken souls intertwining our bodies where our hands cling to one another. In a way, it feels like our intertwined hands are the only thing keeping us together.

But I feel a shift after I tell Langston everything I remember. He doesn't believe me. *Why should he?* We almost always lie to each other. At the very least, we withhold the truth, keep our secrets, or tell half-truths when we share information with each other.

In this instance, though, I'm telling him the truth. Usually, it wouldn't matter if he believed me or not, but our survival depends on help from each other. The only way we are getting out of here is together.

Langston needs to believe me. He needs to trust that what I'm telling him about our current situation is the truth. And I need to trust him.

"Ask me a question."

Langston looks down at me, confused.

"I've already asked you about what you remember."

"No, I mean, ask me our nightly question. You ask me a question, and I'll ask you."

"We don't need to play our game tonight. You need to rest and—"

"No, we need to play our game." I sit up abruptly, looking him in the eyes so he knows how serious I am. "We need to play."

He looks stunned. His mouth has dropped, and he's speechless.

"I'll ask my question first, if that's easier."

He searches my eyes, trying to understand why I'm asking. Finally, he realizes why I'm insisting on playing. This is a game of trust. We need to regain some of the trust we once had as kids. It's the only way we'll survive.

He nods, telling me to go ahead.

"Why are you married to Phoenix?" I ask a tough question, one I need to know the answer to. If he answers, it will mean he wants to earn my trust the same way I do his.

"I can't, huntress. I can't tell you the whole truth."

"Then, tell me part of the truth. Tell me what you can. Don't lie to me. We need to relearn some trust if we are going to survive, if we are going to get out of here, together. We are on the same side for now."

"Are we?"

I nod as I look down at our joined hands. Langston stares too.

"I'm married to Phoenix because I needed her."

I frown as I stare up at him, not understanding. "You needed her as in you needed someone who cared about you? Someone you could be romantic with? Someone to love?"

"I've never experienced romantic love. Not like you and Waylon. I needed Phoenix's help with an outside matter. She was the only person who could help me."

"You mean you needed to marry a Dunn to go after the treasure?"

"That was an added bonus, but it wasn't the reason I married her."

I search his eyes for the rest of the truth, but I know this is as much as I'm going to get from him. He didn't marry Phoenix because he loves her. He didn't marry her so that he could go after the treasure. *Why did he marry her?* My brain is flooding with possibilities, but none of them make sense to me.

"Thank you for what you told me." I smile weakly as I stare back at our hands, wishing that his words would have brought us closer together instead of the opposite.

"I've never loved anyone, Liesel. The only woman I could have ever loved hates me, and so I will never love."

My heart aches at his words. He's talking about me. I'm the woman he could have loved if things were different. I know because he is a man I could have loved if things were different.

I swallow down the pain. "What do you want to know?"

He thinks for a minute, and I think he's going to ask me more about Waylon. "I know you wanted to hurt me. You know Siren is one of the most important people in my life outside of my children. But why? Why did you have to kill her?" His voice shakes as he speaks.

I know for a fact that he doesn't know if Siren is alive or dead. He's just guessing based on her condition and our luck.

His fingers start to pull away from my grasp. It's like he chose this topic because he felt himself getting too close to me and needed a reason to hate me again.

I don't let him pull away.

"Siren isn't dead," I say.

"What? How do you know that?"

I bite my lip, considering my answer.

"Do you have your phone on you? Are you in contact with anyone?" He tries harder to pull away. He's much stronger than me and could rip his hand from mine if he really wanted, but his fingers still cling to mine even as he backs away.

"No, I don't have my phone on me."

"Explain."

I hiss out a breath as my increased heart rate has me breathing too hard and makes my entire body ache. Despite the pain, I face Langston.

"Siren isn't dead because I didn't shoot her."

"What do you mean you didn't shoot her? I watched you. I saw her drop. I—"

"It was all a lie. I was angry. I wanted to hurt you for what you did to Waylon, but as you said, I'm a huntress, not a killer. I couldn't kill her."

"You faked her death?"

I nod slowly. "Siren agreed to help me fake her death. She was pissed at you for kidnapping me and threatening to kill me. Then when I saw Waylon dead in my apartment and Siren saw how devastated I was, she said she would do anything to help me. I needed revenge. I needed you to feel pain like I did, even if it was temporary. So she agreed."

"And Zeke, did he know?"

I nod. "He was pissed for you making Siren suck your cock. So he agreed to play along."

"I wondered why he never retaliated after I did that."

He glares at me, his eyes cutting through me like a blade to butter. And then his eyes soften. "I knew you were never a killer, huntress. I shouldn't have believed my eyes. I should have known to always follow my heart. And I should always count on you lying to me."

I gnaw on my bottom lip, not sure if he's more pissed that I lied and tricked him or relieved that Siren is alive.

His thumb brushes against my bottom lip until I stop chewing on it.

"Thank you for telling me the truth and putting me out of my agony."

"You're welcome."

His other thumb then brushes against the back of my hand as our fingers tighten their grips on each other.

"Now it's my turn to put you out of your agony."

"You're going to tell me the truth about Phoenix?"

"Is that truly the greatest thing causing you agony?"

Yes.

No.

I don't know.

I also want to know why he wants me dead. What sin I did that was too far.

I want to know about his kids.

I want to know why he wants the treasure.

He reads my face and knows that I have too many unanswered questions. Too many to choose from to figure out which one brings me the most pain.

He raises an eyebrow as I once again wince. "I don't think I can reduce your pain with even my most guarded truth."

Langston thinks I shared one of my most important truths with him. I didn't. My honesty about Siren didn't even scratch the surface of the important things I've been lying about. But it was a big enough truth to regain some of Langston's trust. Enough for him to believe me when I say I don't know what happened when I was darted like an animal and raised out of this cell.

His hand is under my chin, lifting it until I'm looking at him.

"Let me help you ease the pain."

"What? How?"

He leans down and brushes his lips against mine, so hesitantly like he thinks I'm going to reject him.

I should—just like I should have rejected every one of his kisses. But I don't want to. His kisses alone are enough to take away most of my pain. His kisses bring my body back to life.

I fall into his lips, demanding more from him. It doesn't take much convincing. His lips consume mine, his tongue pushes into my mouth, and his hand cradles my neck.

As long as his lips are against mine, I forget the burning pain in my lungs, I forget that we are locked away in a tower, and I forget that this is where we will most likely die.

Langston leans back with a sad glimmer in his eyes. It seems he hasn't forgotten about our perilous situation, and he doesn't know how to save us both.

I squeeze his hand, letting him know it's okay. I'm okay. A soft whimper escapes my lips, as his hand glides down the side of my body.

"You're not okay. No matter how much you try to pretend you're not in pain, you are. Let me help you."

I take a slow, deep breath, trying to keep the agony from taking over my every breath, but it's impossible. All I end up doing is grimacing and moaning through every breath.

"You can't help me."

He smirks. "I can."

"How?"

"My kisses make you forget for a split second. Imagine what the rest of my body can do."

I blush, but that can't happen. I can't fuck Langston. I can't even if my body sings to life at the very thought. Even if just imaging him fucking me eases my discomfort, I shouldn't.

"I'm not fucking you, killer."

He grins. "I'm not asking you to fuck me."

"Then, what are you asking?"

He tucks a loose strand of my hair behind my ear. "I'm telling you to let me make you feel good. To let me loose on your body. To let me make you come with my hands, my tongue. Let me help you."

My tongue sweeps across my teeth. My body heats, begging me to say yes. I ache between my legs at the thought of his touch. *How many times have I imagined his touch? Wanted it, but thought it could never happen?*

It's a horrible idea. We are already crossing too many lines. Kissing Langston is one thing. Knowing how it feels for him to make me come is another. My body will crave him in an entirely new way—a way I'll struggle to resist.

"Just this one time?" I ask.

He nods slowly, as his tongue runs over his bottom lip. It's clear how much he wants me to say yes, even though I don't know what he's going to get out of this. He doesn't get to fuck me. He doesn't get to feel any pleasure outside of giving me pleasure.

I smile seductively. "You can help me—that is if you are capable of making me come."

He grins back. "Challenge accepted."

13

LANGSTON

LIESEL AGREED to let me touch her. To make her feel good. To make her come.

It's something I've dreamed about a million times but knew it would never happen. I'm in a state of shock that she said yes.

I'm in a state of shock about a lot of things. Siren is alive. Liesel didn't shoot her. It was all a game. I'm beginning to think I'm losing this game that Liesel and I are playing. I thought I held the most important cards, but I was wrong. Liesel holds more power and secrets than I could have ever imagined.

My thoughts on changing the game will have to wait. Right now, all I can think about is Liesel.

I wish we had a bed, something I could worship her body and pamper her in. Instead, all I have is a cold, rough floor.

Liesel smiles weakly up at me, and I realize it doesn't matter where we are. It doesn't matter the circumstances—all that matters is I have her.

I lean down and kiss her again. Her lips part automatically, and a soft moan purrs into my mouth as I kiss her. I can't believe how she lets me kiss her without asking, like this is the most natural thing in the world.

But just as the kiss deepens, Liesel pulls away. "What about Phoenix? I won't help you cheat on your wife. I won't be the other woman, even for one night. It's one thing to participate in a wild sex game while you're married. This is different."

I knew she'd have doubts about this if I let her think too much. Apparently, my kisses aren't as powerful as I thought.

I frown. "I don't love Phoenix. We are married but only out of necessity, not because we have that kind of relationship. Whatever we do tonight or any other night isn't cheating, and Phoenix knows that." I wish I could tell her that Phoenix and I aren't really married, but that would be another lie. And I'm tired of lying to Liesel if I don't have to.

She hesitates. "I wish I knew why you married her."

"I wish I could tell you."

"But you don't trust me?"

"I trust you more than you realize."

We stare at each other, our eyes getting glimpses into each other's souls. I do trust Liesel—and that's the problem. I trust her when I shouldn't. I want her when I shouldn't. I care about her when I shouldn't.

She grabs the back of my neck and pulls me back into a kiss. This time I know there won't be any more doubts. There won't be any more hesitation on either of our parts.

We've been so close to this before. So close to crossing beyond kissing. I've wanted to touch her, to taste her for so fucking long.

So many times, things have stopped us before. Our history. Our hate. Phoenix. Waylon. That stupid game. Our pride.

There will be no interruptions this time—no one to stop us. I don't care who is holding us captive. I won't let them stop us. Nothing can stop me from claiming another part of Liesel that has always been mine.

I devour her lips with everything that I have, ensuring I remember every second, every touch, every warmth of her lips as I kiss her. No one will interrupt us this time, but that doesn't change our future, our destiny. It doesn't mean we will end up together. It doesn't mean our fate has changed. I learned that a long time ago.

I tangle my hand in her hair as I tilt her head back to give me access to her neck. I kiss every inch of her skin and am rewarded with the softest whimpers of pleasure.

Liesel still has her shell up. I'm going to have to do more to break through than just a few kisses. And I'm going to enjoy every moment of persuading her to lower her guard for me, even if it's just for a moment.

As I kiss down her neck, I instinctively grab the zipper of her jacket. I pull it down to give me access to more of her skin and start kissing down her collarbone before I get a glimpse of her bruises again.

I stop mid-kiss.

"Don't stop," Liesel breathes. "Not if the world is on fire. Please, don't stop."

That's all I need.

I know I have to be careful, gentle with her, so I don't hurt her. I know she's still going to want control as much as I will need her to give up all of the power to me. But most importantly, I will make her scream my name so loudly that the men who hold us captive will want to check on us to see what happened.

Carefully, I tilt her back sideways in my arms as I resume kissing her collarbone and then down over the curve of her breast, encased with the black fabric of her bra.

She takes slow, shallow breaths, and I can only hear the hint of labored breathing that still consumes her pain.

I run my hands over her arms until I remove the leather jacket from her body. I roll it up and then place it behind her head as I lay her back on the floor.

She shivers as the cool floor hits her back.

I grin as I kiss her and feel her warming beneath my body hovering over hers.

"More," she breathes when I try to pull away.

"So bossy." I kiss her again and again and again. I could kiss her forever. But the rest of her body is calling me.

As gently as I can, I run my hand down the front of her body until I hit her bra. I push it up until I find the mound of her right nipple, then I circle my thumb over the nub, making it harden beneath my touch.

"Suck it," she says.

I grin against her lips. That was my plan, but I need her to give me some amount of control if I'm going to be able to take her mind away from the pain she's feeling.

I place my finger against her lips as I lower my head to her nipple. "Suck," I command as I push my finger between her lips.

I hover over her nipple, almost giving in to her order but not doing it until she gives in to mine. Her lips wrap around my fingers, and the gasp that leaves my mouth rattles through my body. I try to hide my reaction by taking her nipple into her mouth.

I try to focus on how supple her nipple is, how incredible it is to be the one making her whimper. But all I can think about is how much of a mistake it was to have her suck my fingers, because now my cock is rock hard and jealous.

She grins around my fingers, knowing the exact reaction she's provoking in me. I pull my fingers from her mouth, and then I swirl them around her other nipple. She cries out in pleasure from my touch.

My eyes rake down her body, watching her every reaction. Goosebumps are all over her arms and stomach. She's still cold.

I want to press my body over hers to keep her warm, but I don't want to hurt her.

Liesel sees the hesitation in my eyes.

"Don't hold back."

I groan. I want to do as she says, but she wouldn't survive if I did. Instead, all I can do is give her the impression that I'm not holding back.

I kiss down her body, even over her bruises, trying to warm her up as I move closer to her black panties. I grab them with my teeth and rip them down her legs to her ankles. Then I gasp at the sight of her pussy so close, so tempting, so mine.

"Lick my clit," Liesel says, still clinging to her control.

She doesn't understand that her body is mine. Even though I've never touched her, I've watched Waylon touch her, other men have her. I've studied her body and know what she wants, what she needs.

She thinks she needs to be in control to come, just like I do. The trauma we have both experienced makes it difficult to trust someone else with our bodies. The only way we allow another to be intimate is if we keep that control.

We aren't even fucking and we are already battling.

I want to take complete control. I want to cover her mouth so she can no longer give me orders. I want to tie her up so she physically can't persuade me to her will.

But I decide on a different route.

I kiss up her legs, moving closer to her clit. I will lick her as she commanded, but I'll take my time.

"Langston," she whines, needing me.

I glance between her legs; she's not ready for me to touch her there yet, as much as she thinks. My first kiss of her clit is going to be explosive. It needs to be in order for her to forget the pain in her chest.

I kiss her upper thigh, the closest I've gotten to following her order.

Her hands grab my hair, and she pushes my head to where she wants me.

I smirk, and her eyes twinkle.

"Lick me, or I'll stop this."

I act like I'm going to move away and stop this.

She growls.

I chuckle.

And then I take her by surprise and do what she asks—I lick her clit.

She moans like I just gave her an orgasm with the single lick. Touching her here is everything I've ever imagined. She's not touching me, stroking me, and I won't be fucking her with my cock, but damn do I feel everything she's feeling.

I lick her again, stroking my tongue over her sensitive bud.

She grips my hair tighter.

I've always enjoyed pleasuring a woman, having my head buried between her legs, but it's always been a prelude to what comes next. But this—this is the most incredible thing I've ever been a part of.

Her legs buckle as I move my tongue in circles around her clit.

She starts to speak, I'm sure to give me another order. But I'm in control of her body now.

I slide a finger to her entrance before she has a chance to speak.

Her breath catches as she waits for me to enter her.

One second. Two seconds. Three...

And then I push a finger inside. She arches her back,

taking all of me in as I continue to lick, rippling through her nerve endings.

I push a second, then a third finger inside her, knowing she wants to be stretched—that she would take my entire body inside her if she could. She wants me. She's desperate for me.

I have no doubt that if I asked to fuck her right now, she'd accept. But that will have to wait for another time. Until I have no doubt it's what she wants. Until I can take her again and again and again. Until she's fully mine.

Something I doubt will ever happen.

So I'll savor this, and it will have to be enough. This is the most I will ever get of her.

I slide my fingers in and out of her as I lick, tasting every sweet drop as I bring her closer to the edge.

"Not yet, huntress."

She moans, and I know she wants to protest. To order me to finish, to make her come but she can't speak. All she can do is moan and whimper.

I continue to work her body, learning even more about her. How much pressure she likes. How deep she likes my fingers. How fast, how slow. I memorize everything about her body.

I feel her getting close. Her muscles are tightening around my fingers. Her breath is speeding. I bring her right to the edge, and then I stop everything.

Her eyes glare at me, and she takes a couple of breaths, trying to regain her speech. "Lang—"

I start again, sending a million shots of electricity through her body as I lick, suck, and slide into her.

Her eyes roll back as she grips onto my head, my shoulders, any part of me she can squeeze.

"Say my name, huntress. I want to hear you scream my name when you come," I order in between licks.

She purses her lips. She's so close, so fucking close.

I look into her eyes, and I know she's not feeling the pain. She's not struggling or fighting for control. She's here with me. Nowhere else. She's not having nightmares of previous terrors. She's basking in how good her body feels for once when she lets someone else take the reins.

But I won't let her come, not until she's given me everything she can give. Not until she gives me what's mine.

"Say it," I whisper as I suck and kiss her clit.

She bites her lip, most likely trying to hold back from screaming my name. From giving into my command. From giving me any control.

Liesel is so close to coming, but I don't think I've won our little battle. She kept her control as much as I battled to take it.

And then, I hear her whimper—the softest, sweetest sound.

"Killer," she moans.

I grin as I push her over the edge with my tongue. Her orgasm explodes around my fingers and ricochets off the walls of the tower.

"Langston," she cries as she comes back down, her body slowing from her high.

We stare at each other at the realization of what just happened. We both surrendered some control. We both claimed something from the other.

One of the many reasons we never thought we could be together was because of our joint need for control. We both thought we needed it above everything else, so we chose partners who were willing to give up control in the bedroom.

This changed things.

Liesel's eyes grow heavy, as I pull her into my lap and stroke her face.

I unroll my jacket that was lying underneath her and drape it over her body to try and warm her. Then I lean my head back against the wall, and I try to sleep, hoping that I took away her pain at least for a few hours.

From her soft snores, it seems that I have.

I hardly remember a time I was happier. But I also know in an instant that I made a mistake. I still hate Liesel for what she did. There is no amount of forgiveness that will change my feelings about her sin.

For a moment, I thought Liesel was truly mine. I thought things could change, and I could have her, but it was a mistake. I shouldn't have touched her, and yet, I don't regret a thing.

Suddenly, I feel a sharp pain in my arm. I look up and see a shadow standing in the window as I once again lose consciousness.

14

LIESEL

I WAKE up with a huge smile on my face. I've never slept so soundly and content in my life, even though I'm sleeping on a gross stone floor.

I stretch my arms over my head instinctively before cringing at the pain in my side. In my bliss, I've forgotten that I'm still injured.

I move Langston's leather jacket aside to look at my injured ribs. I'm still purple and green and sore, but the pain isn't as sharp as yesterday. Today will be much better.

Still, I wish I could remember. It could give us some clue of how to escape. And I hate not remembering any part of my life. It feels like I've been violated in some way, even though I've only been hit in the ribs.

Speaking of violated—my mind goes to what Langston did, and I blush. I've wanted to know what it would feel like to have his lips on me for so long. It's hard to believe that it was real and not a dream—a wonderful reality.

I wasn't sure we could exist together. We're both too stubborn, too dominant, too controlling. I was right and wrong. Both of us needing control made it more exciting, made us more equals, and yet for the first time—I felt comfortable with a man when he took control. That's never happened before.

I roll over, searching for Langston, but find the spot next to me bare.

I sit up abruptly, gripping the jacket to my chest.

The room is dark, but I can see enough to know I'm alone.

"Langston?" I say into the darkness.

As expected, he doesn't speak because he's not here.

I stare up at the dark wall, finding the window high up. I don't see anyone, but I know he's been taken.

I slip the jacket on and zip it up before I start shouting, like that is somehow going to help.

"Langston! Don't you dare hurt him!"

I pound my fists into the wall. "Take me instead!"

There is no answer.

I look around the room for a door, or any other option to escape that may have appeared in the last five seconds. But of course, there isn't another means of escaping.

My options are to break through a wall, dig out underneath the wall, or climb out.

I'm not strong enough to break or dig out. My only option to try and reach Langston is to climb out.

I grip my side. It was hard enough when Langston gave me a boost, I was uninjured, and Langston was below to catch me. This is going to be impossible.

I stare up at the wall, more determined than ever.

I don't know what Langston is going through—torture, agony, rape. *Is he hanging onto the edge of death? Or is he spilling secrets to stay alive and return home to his kids?*

I have to get to Langston. I have to find a way to rescue him.

I grab onto the wall without another thought and begin

to climb. I don't think about failing. I don't think about waiting until the light shines and makes it easier; there isn't a moment to wait. I don't think about falling and hurting myself. I just climb.

I'm completely focused on my task of inching myself higher and higher. My side aches and burns with each movement, but I don't care. Langston won't die, not this way. I can't let him.

So I keep climbing.

I've made it two-thirds of the way up the wall when I hear the window open. I try to look up, but it's hard to look without loosening my grip on the wall.

I consider speaking, but it's still dark, and I'm not sure whoever is at the window can see me climbing the wall. So I freeze.

I watch as a blob is lowered down next to me—Langston.

I stop breathing as I watch his lifeless body lower. The rope holding him breaks halfway down, and he drops to the floor.

I shriek.

I look up, but whoever is at the window is gone. Now's my chance to climb up and escape, but then I look back down at Langston.

There is no way I can leave him.

I start to climb back down quickly until I'm about four feet from the floor, then I drop.

"Langston!" I run to him.

He doesn't move or make a sound as I approach.

"Langston!" I shout again as I try to look him over for any injuries. I find none on a quick inspection, which gives me enough courage to flip him over onto his back without worrying too much about injuring his head.

I hear his barely audible breaths and sigh in relief.

"Langston, wake up."

He moans as I tap his cheek, but I know he won't awaken until whatever drugs are in his system have worn off.

I look him over carefully, but I find no bruises, no blood, no new injuries. He even has a new T-shirt on, and his pants are intact.

All I can do is cradle him in my arms and wait.

———

The sun flickers in before Langston wakes up. I've been holding him in my arms for the last couple of hours, studying everything about his body. I have my suspicions about where he's injured, but I won't know for sure until he's awake.

"Langston?" My heart clenches as his eyes open. I've been worried all night about what happened to him, but I also know that he's going to be in pain now that he's awake. He might even remember the torture he went through. And watching him go through that pain is going to hurt.

"There you are, beautiful."

I run my hand through his locks as I smile down at him. "You must still be drugged up to call me beautiful."

He shakes his head. "You're always the most beautiful woman in any room, my huntress."

I blush. I'm not used to compliments coming from him.

"How are you feeling?" My smile drops, and a look of concern crosses my face. I'm hoping that I'm wrong—that he's not injured. That they just questioned him and then threw him back in this tower with me.

"Better, now that I'm in your arms."

A flicker of a smile returns to my face as I stroke his face. He grabs my hand, and I can tell his intention is to kiss the back of my hand, but the rough growl he lets out instead rips through my chest.

I grab his arm and hold it against his chest to keep him from moving it.

"Hold still."

Langston tries to sit up, but I push his chest, trying to get him to stay down.

He groans. "I need to sit up and figure out where I'm hurt."

"No, you need to lie down and relax while I work on fixing your shoulder and finding all your injuries."

"I need—"

"Lie down," I growl with a seriousness to my tone that finally makes him lie back down.

"You're bossy when you're concerned." He smiles so wide his dimple shows.

"And you make a terrible patient."

I hold his arm against his chest, suspecting that it's popped out of the socket.

"Try moving your left arm, slowly."

He does and immediately hisses.

Shit—both arms are injured.

He starts trying to sit up again and fuss with his arms.

"Stop moving." My eyes bulge at him, my voice stern. I try to hold his arms against his chest in one place as I look at his legs.

"Now, trying moving each of your legs slowly."

He lifts the right leg without any pain and then repeats the same process with the left leg.

"Legs seem fine," Langston says.

I nod.

"I think your shoulders are out of their sockets."

He shakes his head. "Just the right shoulder. The left hurts more in the elbow."

I examine both arms. I don't know what a dislocated shoulder or elbow looks like, so I have no idea how to verify it. And if either of his arms is dislocated, I have no idea how to pop it back into place.

He smiles up at me with a knowing look.

"What?"

"You're adorable when you're concerned about me."

"I'm not—" But I stop myself, because of course, I'm concerned about him. "Do you remember what happened up there?"

His smile drops. "No. I remember holding you in my arms. I remember the sounds you made when you came."

I blush.

"But, I don't remember anything after the drugs entered my system."

We both stare at each other, locking eyes now that we've been through a similar situation. Langston knows that I truly don't remember anything from being tortured, just like he doesn't remember.

"I'm sorry I doubted you," he says.

"Don't be, you had every reason. Just like I have every reason not to trust you—you're still planning on killing me at the end of all of this, after all."

Langston frowns but doesn't correct me.

"What do I need to do about your shoulder and elbow?"

"Nothing."

"Nothing? But your shoulder is dislocated, and your elbow is in pain. Shouldn't I pop it back in place or something?"

He grins at me. "Are you going to let me sit up yet, or do I have to wrestle you until you are pinned underneath me? I'd enjoy either."

I roll my eyes and then put my hands at his back, helping him up.

"Kiss me," he says.

I blink rapidly, my mouth agape. I want to kiss him. I

want to do more than kiss him, but I don't understand where we stand. Every time I kiss him, touch him, get closer to him, I lose a little more of myself to him. I vowed a long time ago I'd never let a man have a claim to any part of me, especially not Langston.

He sighs and is about to give up on me, when I grab his head, turn him to me, and kiss him without any more doubts entering my head.

As soon as his lips hit mine, I'm lost to a fairytale land that only exists when I'm kissing this man. I don't understand how my world can be so perfect only if his lips are pressed against mine. They are soft, warm and oddly comforting, while also being exciting and passionate. They send my heart into a flurry of heartbeats.

With my eyes closed, my tongue pushing into his mouth, and our lips locked, I forget where I am or how few moments we might have left in this world. None of that matters because I'm happier than I can ever remember.

I hear a pop, and I try to pull away, afraid that Langston got hit with another dart and will soon drop. But Langston grabs my bottom lip with his teeth and sucks, keeping my lips locked to his. I melt and cradle his head, hoping I'm not about to lose him to the pull of drugs once again.

Finally, he lets me pull away.

"Thank you," he says.

I raise an eyebrow, not understanding.

"Don't thank me for a kiss."

His eyes cut down to his right arm. "Thanks for the distraction while I popped my shoulder back into place. Your kisses are better than any pain medication."

My eyes widen. "You popped your arm back into place?! You should have told me that was what you were doing."

"Why? Because you would have offered to suck my cock?" he teases.

"You wish." Although, my body heats at the idea of sucking his cock. My mouth waters and my hands itch to feel his long, thick cock in my hand.

"What are you thinking about?" Langston asks, but from his smug expression, it seems he's learned how to read my mind again.

"I'm thinking about how much of an arrogant ass you are."

"Sure, you are." His eyes twinkle at me. "Now, help me get my shirt off so I can use it as a sling."

I suck in a breath and hold it while I grab the hem of his shirt. Maybe if I hold my breath, I'll be immune to being turned on by his rock hard abs. I lift his shirt up his torso and then help him move his left then right arm through the sleeves. He doesn't wince once; he just stares at me as if he's seeing me clearly for the first time.

"What are you looking at?"

He shakes his head, clearing away his thoughts. "Help me tie it up as a sling for my right arm."

"What about your left?"

"It's just my elbow—probably a bruise or strain, I don't think it's dislocated. My right is the one that needs rest the most."

I nod, trusting his own judgment of his body. He's lived his life fighting and getting hurt with fists, bullets, and knives. I'm sure this is normal for him, but it's not for me. This isn't the life I wanted, but it was the life I was always destined to have.

I reach around his back to loop the shirt around and then tie it up on his left shoulder, careful not to brush my hand against his firm chest. Once I've tied the shirt, I help him place his right hand into the makeshift sling.

"You're good at that," I say.

"Good at what?"

"Not showing pain." But then he's been practicing not showing pain since he was five, long before he joined Enzo and his team.

"You make it infinitely easier, but then physical pain is easy to hide. It's the emotional pain that I struggle to keep hidden."

"Where did you and I go so wrong? How did we end up here—hating each other so thoroughly?"

"You're lying if you think we hate each other. We are supposed to hate each other, but that doesn't mean that we do," he says.

Langston's right. Despite him taking everything from me, I could never hate him. And despite whatever horrors he thinks I've done to him, he could never hate me.

"What are we going to do about our predicament?" I ask.

"We should figure out who our enemy is; then we will have the best idea of how to fight him."

"I wish we had something we could use as a shield to keep from being hit by the darts."

"I won't let anyone else drug you. I'll shield you," he promises.

He takes my hand with his left and once again grips it. I wish his words were true. Just like I wish there weren't any lies between us. I wish I could trust him with all of the truths I possess. I wish he could trust me with his.

"So, enemies? Should we go through our list of anyone we can possibly think of?" I ask, bringing the subject back to reality. As much as I want Langston to be my knight in shining armor, he can't be.

"Sure."

Langston scoots back until he's leaning against the wall, and I sit cross-legged in front of him. I'm not at as good as him at hiding my pain, but I try my best to stifle a groan.

"Liesel, are you—"

"I'm fine," I say sternly, not letting him redirect the conversation again.

He narrows his eyes at me.

"So people in my life who might do something like this are Enzo and Kai as retaliation against what I did to Siren if she hasn't come forward and told them the truth."

"Why would they kidnap me?" He raises an eyebrow.

"Okay fine, they wouldn't. Waylon doesn't have a lot of family that would retaliate for his death, but he does have several loyal employees. Nolan Price, his campaign manager, also used to work at his law office. I've always been suspicious of him. There are other men at the law office who were close to Waylon, who didn't think highly of me: Laurence and Christopher. I don't know about the enemies my father made, but I'm sure there are plenty. And then, of course, there are the countless strangers who think they have a right to the money my father hid."

Still such a strange thing to me—my father hid away a mountain of treasure, told me not to find it, and then made public the fact that said money exists. There has to be something I'm missing, something I don't understand. That or my father is just a cruel, conniving man who wanted to ruin my life.

"What about Maxwell?"

I frown. "Maxwell? My bodyguard? He works for me. He doesn't know about the money. He didn't really care about Waylon. Why would he go after us?"

"Just a suspicion. He was more skilled than he let on. He didn't always use his skills. Instead, he chose to pretend he was just an ordinary bodyguard and didn't have training. But that man could rival most of the men we hire."

"Hmm, how did I miss that?"

"Maxwell is an attractive man who is good at manipulating people. It was easy to miss when you spend your time drooling over him."

"Are you jealous of Max?" I bite my lip as I smile brightly, loving that Langston is jealous of Maxwell.

"Max? My point exactly, you didn't even call him by his full name. Clearly, you had a soft spot for him, which would make it easy for him to attack us."

I roll my eyes. "You're jealous of Max. I love it!"

"I'm not jealous of anyone." The vein in his forehead bulges.

He's totally jealous.

"Well, by that logic, Phoenix must have kidnapped us then. She's good looking, more skilled than you give her credit for, and she even married you so she could get close to you and kidnap you."

"Leave Phoenix out of it," Langston growls.

I smirk, happy to have hit a nerve.

"Then who do you think is holding us?" I ask.

He stares off past me as he thinks. For a moment, I think he's figured it out, but then he sighs. "I can't think of a specific person off the top of my head, but maybe that isn't what we need to be focused on. We should be thinking about the traits of the person holding us and how to fight back."

"Hmm, well, what do we know? We know they have a castle with a tower."

"We're deep in a forest."

"How do you know that?"

"The smell of pine."

I take a deep breath, and sure enough, I smell the pine. *How did I miss that before?*

I nod. "Okay, so we are in the forest or mountains somewhere, but not somewhere too cold."

"We know the man likes to hide his identity from us, so

either we know the person or they're afraid we will eventually escape and don't want us to know who they are."

"That makes sense. We also know that they are trying to get information from us, which is why they keep drugging and torturing us. But they don't want us to remember the torture or their identity, hence the drugging."

"We can assume they are after the money or treasure or whatever your father left for you. Am I right?" Langston looks at me like he thinks I might be hiding something from him. I am, just like he is, but not about this.

"I can't think of any other reason."

We both exhale in frustration. We don't seem to have gotten very far.

I yawn. "Should we ask our questions now?"

"No, we should sleep. Tomorrow we need to come up with a plan."

I'm sitting across from him, not sure where I should sleep. *Should I move next to him and curl up on his chest, or should I just curl up in a ball where I'm currently sitting?* I still don't know where we stand.

"No. We need to keep talking until we've shared all our secrets, or until one of us is dead." I refuse to just go to sleep. Answering our questions is just as important as forming a plan. The only way we are going to be able to escape is to rely on one another, and we can't do that if we don't trust each other.

"Fine, ask your question so I can go to sleep."

15

LANGSTON

I WISH I hadn't started our little game. At first, I had all the power—asking questions and demanding answers. I could punish her and take time away from her life. Now that we are trapped and I have no control over her life, the only way I get answers is if I give her an answer myself. And I'm running out of truths I can share with her.

Not to mention I get no benefit from her answers. She either tells me a lie, which only tears us further apart, or she tells me the truth and destroys me with how much we've been hiding from each other. There is no winning. Neither of us will reveal all of our secrets. Neither of us will reveal enough to change our relationship. *So what's the point?*

The only reward from talking to Liesel I can think of is the distraction from my pain. Even though I'm good at hiding how much pain I'm in from other people, it still hurts. My shoulder feels like it's been ripped from my body and thrown haphazardly back together, while my elbow shoots a sharp pain up and down my arm. But when I look at Liesel and listen to her speak, the pain eases.

Liesel purses her lips, considering her question carefully.

"How did you find out you were going to be a father? What went through your head?"

Technically, she asked two questions, but this is an easy one to answer. It's one I like talking about, too, even if I can't reveal the entire truth.

"Phoenix told me I was going to be a father. She was nervous, not sure how I would react. I didn't plan on becoming a father. I didn't plan on Phoenix being my children's mother. But when she told me, sitting nervously next to me on the couch, I didn't care that I wasn't in love with her or that she wasn't my perfect woman. All I cared about was that I was going to be a father."

Liesel smiles at me.

"I was terrified at first. I don't know what it looks like to be a good father. My upbringing wasn't something I would wish on my worst enemies. But the fear slipped away within seconds, and all I felt was overwhelming joy and happiness. My entire life flashed before my life, and I knew this is what I was always meant to do—be a father.

"I vowed in that moment to be the best father I could. I would protect them from the dangers of the world. Show them what it felt like to be loved. Give them a family. Always put them first. Being a father is the greatest accomplishment of my life."

"From what I can tell, you've been a great father," she says.

I nod. "Thank you."

She leans back on her elbows and looks up as the moon reflects off her blonde hair and hazel eyes.

"What about you? How did you feel when you found out you were going to be a mother?"

I already know the answer. She's already told me before, but it gives her a chance to talk about her feelings for the child she gave up.

"I never wanted to be a mother, and the world agreed. There wasn't anything to feel beyond some sadness at the situation. Unlike you, I knew I wasn't cut out to be a mother. The choice to give up my child was easy."

Liesel hides her emotions well. She's feeling more that she isn't telling me, but I won't force her to reveal more tonight.

"Ready to sleep?"

She nods.

I start inching down the wall, assuming she'll curl up next to me, but as I lie down on the floor, I find Liesel already curled up on her side with her eyes closed.

I sigh. I guess she won't be sleeping next to me, after all. And it seems our stupid questions game has once again pushed us apart instead of bringing us closer together. I should be happy; we've been growing too close these last few days, far too close.

Especially when the end of our relationship has always been fated—with one of us dead.

———

My sleep is restless between the cool floor, my aching shoulder, and Liesel sleeping so far away. I shouldn't be so needy. I shouldn't need Liesel snuggled up against me in order to sleep. I shouldn't need her at all.

And yet, in the short time we've been together, I've found myself needing her more and more. I'm going to have to detox from her if we ever get out of here.

I roll over and groan, forgetting that my left arm is just as injured as my right. I flip back onto my back and sigh. There is no way I'm going to get any sleep. I should start coming up with a plan to get out of here, but honestly, I can't think with the pain surging through my body. There is nothing to distract me now.

"Hmmm," I hear Liesel hum, and I glance over through the dark to where she's asleep on the floor.

I smile. I may not get to hold her in my arms, but at least I can listen to her while she sleeps.

The humming changes into a soft snore. I'm thankful that she can sleep. It will be easier to face tomorrow if she's rested.

"Are you awake?" she asks suddenly.

"Yes, but I'm fine. You should go back to sleep, Liesel."

Silence. I assume she's closed her eyes and is drifting back to sleep. She probably won't even remember waking up in the morning.

"Does this hurt?" she asks, as she touches my left arm.

I nod.

Even in the dark of night, I can see her brow furrow, and her lips turn downward.

"Don't look so sad on my account. I'm fine, huntress."

"If you were fine, you'd be asleep. How bad is the pain?"

"Not bad enough that you need to worry." I look at her chest. "How is your pain?"

"You can't change the subject that easily. We are talking about you, not me."

"I'd be better if you slept on my chest; that way, I can listen to your soft snore easier while I fall asleep."

"I don't snore," Liesel pouts.

I grin. "You do, too. Now come here." I hold out my left arm for her to snuggle against my chest. It will hurt my arm, but I don't give a damn about that. All I want is to feel her warm body against mine.

She moves to lay on my chest and then hesitates. "I don't want to hurt you."

"You won't." Although, that's a lie. She's already hurt me

in every way that she can. It will hurt to have her lying on my arm all night, but not as much as not having her lie on my arm.

Slowly, she lowers herself down until her head is resting on my chest. My left arm hugs around her, and I force myself not to grimace when some of her weight pushes back on my arm.

"I think I'm beginning to figure out your tells," she says.

"What do you mean?"

"I can tell when you are hiding your pain. You don't show the usual reactions. You try to overcompensate so no one knows you're hurting. You smile instead of grimace. You talk instead of suffering in silence. You ask me to snuggle with you instead of asking me to hold you. You soften instead of stiffening as a way to cushion the pain. You don't have to hide your pain from me. I understand it more than anyone. I know how strong you are."

"You think I hide my pain because I'll look weak if I don't?"

She thinks for a moment, then nods.

"I hide my pain because I don't want to worry you. I don't want to be taken care of. It's the same reason you don't want me to know about your pain. If I'm nice to you, it erases some of our history, some of the evil things we've done to each other." I pause. "Taking care of each other now while we are under duress and have no one else to rely on doesn't change anything between us. After we get out of here, we'll go back to being enemies. Deal?"

She smiles softly. "Deal. Now, let me help distract you from the pain."

I pull her close to me, assuming she means by snuggling or, if I'm really lucky, by kissing me.

Instead, she lifts herself off my chest.

"Where are you going?" I reach out to tug her back down.

"You have to promise to do exactly what I say. You can't give me any orders. You can't boss me around. You have to promise to relax and just let me have all the control. Can you do that?"

My eyes narrow as I study her. I don't know what she's talking about.

"I don't like giving up control."

"You need to try if you want me to help to distract you."

"Liesel, I know you are trying to be coy, but I really don't know what you are talking about. So please just say it."

Her hand dances down my chest and then stops just above the waistband of my pants.

"I want to repay the pleasure you gave me last night. But only if you submit to me." Her eyes are heated, but I know there's some fear. Each time we cross the line, we inch closer and closer to the point of no return. But the fear isn't just about us growing too close; it's also about hurting each other.

Because of her past, she needs complete control when she's with a man. Me having any control when I touched her was just because of how I knew her body, not because she trusted me. Now, she needs that control back.

I grab her wrist, stopping her. "I don't need you to repay me. What I gave you I did because I enjoyed it."

"I know. Let me enjoy your body. Give me the control." Her voice is soft but certain.

I can't believe I'm trying to turn this woman down. I want her badly. My cock is already hard, and she hasn't even touched me. I've dreamed of her touching me so many times, but I don't know how many more times we can touch and kiss each other without actually fucking. It's going to drive me mad, even if I'm in no shape to fuck her tonight.

She moves her free hand over my crotch, feeling how hard I am.

"Huntress," my voice sounds in a warning. If she starts this, there is no going back. Another layer of protection will be stripped from us. This will continue to change and morph our relationship. More feelings will be involved than before.

Liesel Dunn is the one woman I've always wanted to fuck, and yet, I can't. Any time we get close to fucking, I remember why we shouldn't. Why I can't, we can't. But my resolve is slipping. I don't have much self-control left. And if I ever claim her as mine, I don't know if I'll be strong enough to do what has to be done.

"Let me touch you. Let me make you feel good. Let me help you forget."

She squeezes through my pants to my cock. I close my eyes, not believing how good it feels to have her touch me even through the fabric of my pants.

I should say no. I shouldn't give her any more control. I shouldn't push us closer to our inevitable end.

But there is no way I can refuse her, no way I can turn her down.

"You aren't fighting fair," I say, still gripping her wrist while her other hand teases me. I'm sure I could overpower her and capture both of her hands with my one hand to make her stop, but I don't want to.

"Give me control. Don't fight me. Don't order me. I'd tie you up to ensure you can't control me, but with one arm in a sling and the other injured, I don't think I need to. Give me your word." She stops rubbing and waits for my answer.

She tells me to give up control, but in this moment, the decision is entirely mine.

I release her hand as I exhale a shaky breath.

She notices and smiles, but I can see that her breathing is just as erratic as mine. She leans forward and kisses me. At first, the kiss is hesitant, like I'm not sure she wants this or is going to be able to take complete control. But then she grips my hair and forces my head back, kissing me roughly. Our tongues tangle, along with our moans.

"Stand up," Liesel says when she pulls back.

I frown. I don't want to stand. I'm exhausted.

She gives me a warning look to obey her, or this ends.

I start to place my hand down to ease myself up, when she hooks her arm under mine and helps me. Then we are both standing.

She smiles at me. "Good boy."

I growl. "I'm not a dog."

She laughs and rewards me with a passionate kiss that almost knocks me off balance. She grabs onto my hair to steady me, and I realize she has even more control with me standing weakly in front of her.

She breaks the kiss and starts kissing my neck, my chest, and then she kneels in front of me.

"Liesel, you don't—"

"I'm in control. I don't want to hear you speak unless you're moaning my name."

She grips my pants and yanks them down before licking her lips and staring at my naked body. My cock is hard and straining toward her. I want nothing more than to grab her hair and slide my cock down her throat, but she's in control, and I won't dare hurt her. Not in this way. She's been hurt by too many men. If there is one thing I want to show her is that some men can be trusted with her body. She just has to learn how to choose the right ones.

She leans forward with her eyes on me as her lips press a kiss to the tip of my cock. The single touch proves this is going to take all of my restraint to not take control. She's not the only person who has gone through trauma. Ours might be different, but it still controls us both the same—with flashes of nightmares, need for power, and inability to love.

"I want you, killer. Don't ever think I don't. Tell me that

you want me," she whispers as she wraps her hand around my cock.

"I want you too, huntress." I don't speak because she commands me to, but because it's the truth.

I want to grab her. I want to wrap her legs around my waist and fuck her against the wall. Against the floor. With her riding on top of me. But I know that can't happen. I won't let our first time be under duress in this cramp tower. She deserves better than that. Better than me. Better than any man.

"Grab my hair," she says with her lips pressed against my cock.

"If I grab your hair, I'm not sure I'm going to be able to hold back," I croak out. I'm afraid I'll slam her head and pump her mouth over me too hard as I thrust into her mouth.

She grins. "Try to keep up with me."

Then she thrusts her mouth over my cock, taking all of me into her mouth until I'm halfway down her throat. I grip her hair, more to keep from falling over than to pump her head over my shaft.

And then she's sliding her mouth over me. Her pace is wicked as she hungrily slides her mouth and hand over my length. Her tongue swirls around the tip before plunging me back into her throat.

She takes complete control over my body, something I'm not used to. When I'm with other women, they like a man in power, and I like tying them up and being the violent monster they all think I am.

But watching Liesel on her knees in front of me, stroking me and me completely at her mercy—if I ever thought I could fall in love with a woman, I would right now.

Her eyes flirt up at me, knowing that even if I wanted to take control, I couldn't. She holds all the power. I'm weak for her, and I've never enjoyed feeling weak more than I do right now.

"Huntress," I warn through a rasp in my throat.

I don't know if she'll swallow my seed, let me come on her body, or spit it out. And for once, I'm happy to let her choose.

I grip her head harder as her she lets a hint of her teeth scrape against my sensitive skin. I feel like a feral animal as she pumps over me. She's awakened a wildness in me I didn't know existed—at least, not when I'm with a woman.

"Liesel!" I scream as I pump my cum between her lips, spilling the salty liquid onto her tongue. She takes every drop I give her as I shudder. Then she swallows my cum down her throat, but she doesn't remove her mouth from my cock. She takes her time sucking every last drop and then licking me clean.

I still grip her hair as she continues to kneel in front of me. I'm too dizzy and out of my mind to stand on my own.

She smirks, reveling in the effect she has on me. She grabs my hand as she stands and kisses me softly on the lips. She's afraid if she kisses me too hard, I'll faint, and I probably would.

"Now, we can sleep."

She leads me by the hand back to the spot where we've slept every night, and then she helps me to sit before retrieving my pants and tossing them to me. I wiggle them back on one-handed while she sits down next to me.

"Thank you," I say as the hormones flow through my body, easing any pain in either of my arms.

"Don't thank me for letting me take what I wanted."

I lean my head against her forehead, wishing we could truly take what we both want. Wishing our lies aren't so monumental. Wishing our secrets aren't destined to destroy what's left of our relationship. Wishing our fate is different, like what I once thought it could be when we were kids.

"Someday, one of us will take too much," I say.

"I know, but until that day, we should stop fighting what we want. Stop paying for our pasts or worrying about our futures. For now, let's just enjoy what we want from each other."

I hope she's right. I hope we can enjoy what is left of our time together.

She lies down, and I lie down next to her.

"Come here," she says.

I scoot next to her and put my arm out for her to curl up on my chest.

She shakes her head. "You're injured. I'm not sleeping on your arm and hurting you worse."

"You could never hurt me."

"You're wrong. I could hurt you more than you realize. But I don't want to. Sleep on my chest instead."

I frown. "I'll crush you."

She shakes her head. "You said you would give me control."

"Yes, but only when you were making me come."

"You said you'd give me control. That doesn't end yet, and you'll accept that if you ever want my mouth wrapped around your cock again."

My heart stops, but I surrender. Gently, I lay my head down against her soft chest. "Again?"

She blushes, and her eyes twinkle with thoughts of being my dirty girl again.

"I won't deny that I like your body, just like you like mine. It doesn't mean I like you."

"Of course, it doesn't."

"Go to sleep," she commands.

I close my eyes. Liesel has taken away my pain and

replaced it with memories of her sucking my cock. Of her on her knees. Of her saying she wants a repeat.

Again.

I want more. I want to fuck her. Sink into her. Feel the deepest pleasures I can with her. But it's for the best that I don't. My heart and soul wouldn't survive it. She wouldn't survive it. But then again, we have always been destined to destroy each other.

LIESEL

HE'S MINE.

That's the tale my mind tells me as I dream. Langston Pearce is mine. He's my match, my partner, my soulmate. He was always destined to be mine: my best friend, my lover, my husband.

But when I open my eyes, reality hits me hard in the chest. The same chest that Langston is currently lying and drooling on.

Langston isn't mine. He'll never be mine, despite how much I want him. There are countless reasons why Langston will never be mine, why I'll never have him beyond what we've already done.

For one, he's a bastard who has threatened my life.

Two, he's failed over and over when he vowed to protect me.

Three, he's married. Although, I'm still not sure of the exact status or reason for that marriage. He's still married. Unless he divorces, he can never truly be mine.

Four, the only reason he even gives me any time of day is because of the treasure. He still hasn't told me why he wants the money. I suspect to get back at me for whatever horrible thing he thinks I've done.

And five, he killed Waylon.

There is too much to forgive, to forget, and to overcome for us to ever be together. Fucking Langston now would only lead to heartbreak later. But I need to keep all the reasons I can't be with Langston fresh in my mind to fight my overwhelming feelings of lust for him. I've had a taste; that will have to be enough. I'm not sure my heart could take more.

"What are you thinking about so seriously?" Langston says without opening his eyes as he nestles into my chest.

"About how heavy your head is."

He chuckles. "I don't think I'm ever going to get up again. Your chest is too soft."

He rubs his head against my breast.

I roll my eyes, but don't brush him off me. I quite enjoy having him resting on me. I run my hand through his hair.

"How are you feeling?" I ask.

"Horrible. My arms are throbbing, and I have shooting pains up and down my arm all the way through my back."

He moans when I stroke his cheek.

"I'm so sorry. Do you want me to rub your back? Is there something I can do to help?"

He scrunches his face in agony. "I think a repeat of last night is the only way to relieve my pain."

I break out into laughter, and he does the same as I swat him on the head. We both sit up.

"You horny bastard." I playfully hit his chest.

He wiggles his eyebrows. "It was worth a try."

"There's a tray of food and water," I say, pointing to the corner.

Langston tries to get up, but I put a hand on his chest. "I

got it." I walk over and pick up the tray before setting it down on the floor next to us.

Langston looks up, like he can't believe food was lowered without us waking and noticing. I can't believe it either.

Both of our stomachs growl, though, so any discussion of how we slept through the food being lowered will have to wait until we've finished eating.

There's a couple of pieces of dry toast, peanut butter, and bananas. We eat everything on the plate and drink all of the water.

"We need a plan," I say before I finish the last drop of water. We won't survive much longer like this. We are getting fed, yes, but not enough to sustain us. We've both already lost a couple of pounds. Our injuries aren't life-threatening so far, but that doesn't mean it will remain that way for long.

"Do you have any ideas?"

"Yes, actually."

He grins. "My huntress is always the best at coming up with the plans."

"I suspect that we will once again be darted. That seems to be our captor's MO. He doesn't want us to know who he is. I don't know if we can avoid being hit entirely by the darts, but we can pull them out as soon as it hits us, so that hopefully we don't get a full dose, and we can remember more about our torture. Our goal after we are darted and raised should be to gather as much information as we can."

"Your goal should be to run if you can. If you get an opportunity to get out, you take it. Don't worry about me."

I won't agree to that, not unless I think I can get help to rescue Langston.

"I doubt we will have that opportunity unless we can avoid getting hit entirely by the darts. If we are even partially drugged, it will make it hard to run."

"I don't intend for you to be hit with another dart," he says.

I shake my head. "You aren't going to be able to prevent a flying dart from hitting me."

"You vastly underestimate my abilities, huntress."

I smile, sadly. "That's because I've overestimated your abilities before and you failed me."

His face looks crushed. He couldn't prevent me from getting raped. He couldn't keep me safe. From that point on, my life was different.

Langston reaches out and grabs the back of my neck as his thumb strokes my cheek. "There is no reason you should trust me in this. All I can do is apologize for failing you. I was young and stupid and cocky. I'm grown up now and have experienced the world. I won't fail you. If I make a promise to you, I'm going to keep it. Even if it kills me."

Everything inside me wishes I could believe him, but everything is screaming not to trust him.

17

LANGSTON

LIESEL DOESN'T BELIEVE that I'll do anything to protect her, and she shouldn't. But it's a vow I'll keep all the same.

"Maybe we should tell each other everything on our half of the letter? Stop hiding secrets from each other, so we have all the information we need to steer our interrogators astray? Or at least if only one of us survives, we can have the information we need to go after the treasure ourselves," she says, suddenly, completely out of character for her.

"You're willing to give me the information that I've been begging for and threatening your life over, just like that?"

She stills and then blinks. "Yes."

"And how would I trust that anything you said was the truth?"

"You'd know, just like I'd know if you were telling a lie."

I don't know her true motives for wanting to discuss what we know. But even if she wants to tell the truth, it can't happen here.

"First of all, no one is going to die. I won't let that happen."

She sighs. "You aren't God; you can't control everything."

"I can."

She shakes her head with a smile. "Pompous asshole."

"That's me, but we can't talk about the truth of what we know about the treasure. Whoever is holding us might be listening, and no one but the two of us can ever know the truth."

She narrows her eyes, trying to understand what I'm not saying. She still doesn't know the truth of why I want the treasure, why I'm pressing the issue so much, and she'll probably never know.

"You're right. I don't know what I was thinking. I just can't sit down here day after day and wait to be drugged, tortured, and most likely eventually killed."

I know what she means. Even now that we have a sort of plan, I don't want to just sit and wait, filled with an unlimited amount of anxiety. I'm paranoid that every sound is them coming for us—coming to hurt Liesel.

"Then let's not just sit around waiting."

"What do you suggest?" Her cheeks blush, telling me the dirty thoughts she's thinking.

"You want to be honest with one another so we feel like we are fighting on the same side. Then let's be honest. Rattle off random truths. Simple truths that don't really matter but tell us something about each other."

"And if either of us lie?"

"Then, the other gets to steal a kiss." It gives me more incentive to lie than tell the truth, but we are both far more comfortable lying than telling the truth anyway. And Liesel needs more excuses to kiss me. Or maybe she needs an excuse to pull away from me. Either way, I'm going to learn more about her feelings for me this way than if I ask her questions directly.

"I love being a lawyer," she says.

"That, I believe. You always enjoyed arguing with people."

"I do, but as hard as it might be to believe, I also enjoy helping people, whether society says they deserved to be helped or not."

"Hmmm, I never would have taken you to have feelings for other people."

"Are you calling me a liar?" she asks. She's been walking in circles around the room, running her hand along various lines on the bricks, while I sit in the center watching her.

"No, just surprised to find out the ice princess has a heart."

Her eyelashes bat in my direction, like she's trying to hide more of the mystery of who she is.

"I hate my beach house. It's so big, and I prefer the cold of the mountains to the beach. I think I'm going to have to build a new dream house in the mountains."

Her mouth falls open at my words, and I think I heard a little of her heart breaking.

I grin, flashing her my dimple.

Her eyes change in realization. I told a lie so she could decide whether to call me out on it and earn a kiss. Of course, I love my dream house. I love the ocean. I wouldn't trade it for any palace in the world. She knows that. *But does she want to kiss me again in the daylight?*

"I hate the beach house, too. You locked me in a freaking closet. You locked me off from your real home with Phoenix and your kids. The views were horrible. You tainted my dream house by making it my jail cell. I hate it, too."

She holds back a smile as she says it. She's teasing and taunting me just like I did to get a response. But I won't be the first to crack. I won't be the one asking for a kiss. We both already know that I want to kiss her. It's her feelings that I'm trying to figure out.

"I have a favorite child. Atlas is so much more sensible than Rose. I hate how much trouble Rose gets into."

Liesel frowns and shakes her head, knowing once again that I'm lying, but she doesn't say it.

"I think Phoenix and I will become great friends. The best of friends."

Her lie is just as brazen as mine, but once again, I don't call her out on it.

"Good, because I think once you get to know Phoenix, the three of us will enjoy having a threesome."

"Liar."

I grin seductively. "Oh, yea? You think I'm a liar?"

"Yes," she breathes, barely able to get the single word out.

"Do you want to punish me by making me kiss you? Or would you prefer a different punishment?"

She stops circling me. "Stand up."

I do as she says.

"You're a cheating bastard, Langston. You lied on purpose to get a reaction out of me."

"Did I? But then, that's the game. Kiss me or don't. Either way, I'm a tortured man. Kissing you tortures me, dangling so close to what will never be mine. But at least I get to kiss you. Not kissing you breaks my spirit."

"We can't have that."

She walks over to me until we are standing face to face.

"What stops you from wanting me? From wanting to fuck me? From giving in to your lust?"

She purses her gorgeous red lips, that still look like they've been painted red with her favorite lipstick. Her lips have always been the thing I've found most attractive about her. Her mouth is capable of so many wonderful things— sassy comebacks, delicious kisses, and wrapping themselves around my cock.

"You're a married man."

"You've fucked plenty of married men."

"That's true, but…"

"I've told you countless times I'd never get married, and yet here I am—married."

She nods. "That's part of it."

"And if I got divorced, would that change your mind?"

She stops breathing, as do I. "No, we have too much history. I would never want to give you the pleasure of thinking I was yours, even for a night."

Our eyes lock back in our endless battle.

"What would it take?"

"There is nothing that you could give that would make me yours."

I pause at her painful words. Then, I say the only thing that might save me. "Liar."

Her eyes cut back to me, and I grab her hand, yanking her to me until she's pressed against me. "What would it take?"

"More than you are willing to give." And then she presses her lips against mine, most likely to shut me up and end the conversation. But I'll take any kisses she's willing to give, even if she's trying to trick me again.

The kiss is intoxicating, as are all her kisses. I'm so consumed that I almost don't hear the window opening until it's too late, but I hear just in time.

I keep kissing her, ensuring that she can't play my savior. Then, at the very last second, I turn her and take the dart meant for her.

Her eyes widen, and she yanks the dart out of my back as soon as she realizes what I did. She tries to stare up to get a look at the shooter, but I block her. I only have seconds left until I fall unconscious.

"Stay beneath me. Don't let them shoot you, promise me."

I start to fall toward her, and she does her best to catch me. My body is still shielding her.

"I promise," she whispers as we collapse to the floor, with my body covering her.

"What if I told you I love you? That I've always loved you? Would that be enough to make you mine?" I say, as my eyelids grow heavy.

I never hear her response before the world goes black.

LIESEL

WHAT IF I told you I love you?

Langston's words are all I can think about as he collapses on top of me. I should be focused on avoiding any more darts coming my way, but I'm entranced with Langston's words. I wish he could wake up and continue our conversation. There are more pressing issues, though.

Still...

What if Langston did love me? Would that make any difference?

No, it would make things worse.

I glance up just as another dart is sent down toward my chest. I move Langston's arm at the last second, so it enters him instead of me. Rolling his arm so that I can pull the dart out and lay it against my chest, I hope they'll think the dart hit me instead of Langston.

I look up at Langston one last time before I pretend to pass out, and I can't help but brush my lips against his. He doesn't kiss me back, but it doesn't matter. I like the soft touch and smell of him. I like being able to appreciate his body without worrying about how he interprets it.

Langston's silly attempt at getting me to admit feelings toward him didn't go unnoticed. I knew exactly what he was doing when he started the game. The problem is, everything is so damn complicated.

I close my eyes and let my head fall back, pretending to be hit by the dart. A few seconds later, I hear men's voices mumbling above us, but I can't make out what they are saying. A creak of the window and the thump of a rope follows. I so wish I could open my eyes, but I need to wait until we are above ground. That will give me the best chance of learning something that will help us escape.

I wish Langston hadn't been knocked unconscious, that we had removed the dart in time. When I kissed him, I felt nothing back, though. He wouldn't have been able to resist kissing me back if he was still conscious.

Langston's body is lifted up off of me a few minutes later. Despite how hard it was to breathe with Langston on me, I immediately miss the feeling of his body against mine.

Another man lifts me into his brawny arms before I'm set down again. I smell Langston's body immediately, and I know I'm lying on his body.

Before I can worry about damaging Langston's injured arm further, I feel a contraption swinging us in the air. I hold my breath to keep from shrieking as the rig swings hard to the left, nearly knocking us off. Somehow, I resist the urge to grab onto Langston and reveal myself.

The swinging stops as we are plopped on the ground. We are upstairs, above ground, no longer in the tower.

I feel hairy arms beneath my head and legs as I'm once again lifted from the ground, away from Langston. My heart aches at the distance between us. I hope that Langston is being carried right behind me and that we are headed to the same room. I'm not sure I can stand to be apart from him when he's so vulnerable while unconscious, not to mention his hurt arms.

The man carrying me walks for a while. Apparently, wherever he's taking me to be tortured isn't nearby.

A door is kicked open, and I'm desperate to open my eyes to see where I am. But I keep my eyes tightly closed and do everything I can to keep my breathing and heartbeat slow and steady.

I'm plopped down roughly on a couch as if to test if I'm awake. I don't react, even when one of my hands and legs fall off the couch. I let them hang uncomfortably, my body barely staying on the couch.

Footsteps retreat, and then I hear the door close.

Even then, I don't move.

I'm lying on a couch, but I know without opening my eyes that Langston isn't here with me. I'd feel him. It terrifies me where they could be taking him or what they could be torturing him with.

My fear makes me brave enough to open my eyes the tiniest of slits. I'm in a fancy room, in what seems like a castle. The walls are stone, just like the tower we've been kept in, and the furniture looks like it comes from the previous millennia. The couch I'm lying on has gold claw feet, matching the color of the chandelier over my head.

But the room is empty. I open my eyes further and lift my head. It's then I see one of the two doors is open. Through its opening, I see another door with an inset window revealing the outside.

I could run.

Langston told me if I got the opportunity, I should run.

My heart thumps so slowly and loudly in my chest; I'm sure everyone in the house can hear it.

I stare at the door.

Run, I tell myself.

But I don't. I don't even get off the couch. I sit and turn my head to the other door—the closed door, the door I must have been carried through. That's the way to Langston.

I hear Langston's voice in my head. *Run, huntress. Don't worry about me. Save yourself.*

My heart flickers to the closed door.

I should run. I know I should. This might be my only chance. And by running, I could go and get help. I could call Enzo or Kai so they could send a team to rescue Langston.

I don't know how much longer I have until someone comes to check on me. I don't know how many guards are outside the house. I don't know if I'll get this chance again.

I stand, trying to make my decision.

Left to freedom.

Or right to Langston.

The decision ultimately ends up being easy—I run toward the closed door, toward Langston.

I can't save myself without saving him. If I left, they could kill him before I brought anyone to save him, and I couldn't face that.

I get to the closed door and listen carefully for any sign of someone standing guard. I don't hear anyone, but that doesn't mean they aren't there.

Slowly, I open the door wide enough to look down the hallway. I don't find anyone, so I open the door all the way and step through. The hallway is quiet and empty.

I start walking down the hallway, hoping to find Langston or some hint of who is holding us. With any luck, Langston will have woken up by now, and we will be able to sneak out together.

I get to a fork in the hallway. I can continue on straight or turn to the right. There are no people straight ahead, so I push my head forward to look down to the right. It's empty as well.

My gut tells me to go right. There are a lot more doors to the right than straight ahead.

I continue down the hallway as silently as I can, looking for clues of whose house this is or where Langston is. All of the decorations look to be a century or more old and have no personal touches. I wouldn't be surprised if this is a rental property. That, combined with the seemingly lack of security cameras or guards, makes it feel like whoever is holding us doesn't have as much money or skill as we first thought.

I come to the first door and place my ear against it to listen. I don't hear anything, so I continue on.

I do the same to two more doors before I get to one where I hear a gentle moaning sound. I open the door, too quickly, and it makes a creaking sound. But I'm in such a hurry to get to Langston if he's hurt.

Langston is lying on the cold floor, but no one is watching him. They must think since they drugged us that they don't need to stand guard—what fools.

I race over to his side and gently pat his cheek.

"Langston, you have to wake up. We have to get out of here."

I tug on his arm and try to roll him over.

He moans but doesn't open his eyes.

"Sorry about this, but you need to get up."

I take his arm out of the sling and pull hard.

He growls and grips it, his eyes flying open.

I exhale sharply. "We have to get out of here," I repeat.

He looks around, completely confused, but we don't have time to explain or wait until his brain is fully functional again.

"Can you stand?"

"I think so."

He starts to push himself up with one arm but falls.

"I've got you," I say, looping his arm over my shoulders and lifting him up.

He's heavy, and his feet seem barely functional. I won't be able to help him far. Hopefully, his legs will start working soon. If not, we won't make it far without being caught.

"Well, well, how clever you are to have avoided a dart," a man says from the doorway. He's wearing a sharp-looking suit, apparently the king of this castle. It's almost like he's from another time.

He snaps his fingers, and two men run inside and pull Langston from my shoulder.

"Don't hurt him!" I plead as they throw him back down on the ground. He's too drugged up to fight. He can barely even lift his head.

"Well, that depends on you, Miss Dunn," the man in the suit says.

I continue to look at Langston on the floor. I'm completely helpless. I've failed. Now I know how Langston must have felt when he failed to protect me. It's a horrid feeling that creeps up your chest and throat, taking hold of all your senses.

"What do you want?" I ask.

"Come with me, Miss Dunn, and we can discuss what will be done about Mr. Pearce."

I bite my lip and hold back tears as I look at Langston, broken and weak on the floor. I want to run to him, hold him, protect him.

"Promise me if I go with you, you won't hurt him," I say.

The man smiles. "This isn't a negotiation. You are in no position to negotiate."

"You want information from me, yes?"

He shrugs. "From either of you. Whoever tells me what I need gets to live."

I shake my head. "The only way you get the information

you need is if you let him live. Each of us only has half the information. You need both of us."

The man frowns. "I promise I won't hurt him until after we've talked. You have my word."

It's the best I'm going to get, so I take a step to follow him.

"No, Liesel," Langston says, trying to scramble to his feet to come after me.

I refuse to turn and look at him. I'm doing this to save him. I won't let him persuade me to let him suffer in my place with his puppy dog eyes or commanding voice.

The man in the suit looks past me to his two employees. "Make sure he stays here, unharmed until I say otherwise."

I exhale sharply in relief. The man starts walking out of the room, so I follow him like a loyal servant.

He doesn't speak to me as we walk down the hall, and I try to tune out Langston's moans and pleas.

Please, let me be doing the right thing.

The man stops in the original room I was laid down in. He puts his hand out, indicating for me to sit on the couch, so I do. I told him I'd do anything to keep Langston safe, and I will. I'll do anything, and that terrifies me.

I want Langston's kids to grow up with a father—that's the only reason I'm doing this. I don't care about Langston, not really. I just want his secrets, and I don't want to be responsible for making two beautiful children fatherless.

The man shuts the first door, then walks over to the second door that has a view of the outside door. He slowly shuts it, closing off my escape.

"You're very interesting, Miss Dunn."

"I sure am, Mr....?"

He smiles at me. His dark hair is perfectly combed over, his teeth are pearly white, and his sharp jaw is clean-shaven. He looks like he's about to go into a boardroom, not about to interrogate someone for information about stolen treasure.

"I don't think you've earned my name yet, Miss Dunn."

"If you are going to torture me, you might as well call me Liesel."

"Who says I'm going to torture you?" He sits on the arm of the couch and stares at me, completely in control of his pleasant facade.

"Just a guess based on the fact that I was taken against my will, locked in a tower, and the last time you brought me above ground, I ended up with some broken ribs."

"You exaggerate. I doubt your ribs were actually broken."

I narrow my eyes. "You dislocated my friend's arm and injured his elbow."

"Did I?"

"You did."

"Well, Miss Dunn, I prefer to talk over torture, and it seems you will be amenable."

"What do you want with me and Langston?"

"You disappoint me, Miss Dunn. You shouldn't ask questions you already know the answer to."

I frown. "What do I have to do for you to allow Langston to go free?"

"Now, that is a much better question."

"One that you intend to answer, or will you continue to talk in riddles?"

"I'm curious. He took all of the drugs for you, so that you would stay conscious. My men stupidly left you unattended in this room, with a clear escape route. Why didn't you escape and save yourself?"

I tilt my head. "You shouldn't ask questions you already know the answer to."

He cracks up like I'm the funniest thing in the world.

"You're quite amusing, Miss Dunn. I might just keep you for entertainment."

"I don't care what you do with me, as long as Langston goes free."

He purses his lips and puts his hand to his chin as he studies me. "I've done my research on you, and I thought you were a soulless creature who only looked out for yourself, but I'm afraid I was mistaken—you do have a heart."

Now it's my turn to laugh. "I don't have a heart."

"Then, accept my deal. You give me some basic information, and then I'll let you go."

"You'll keep Langston?"

He nods.

"What will you do to him?"

"Whatever it takes to get the information we seek."

I frown.

"And then, we'll kill him."

I gasp.

He smiles, getting more information on me than I might have otherwise admitted. He stands from the arm of the chair and walks over to me, lifting my chin to look at him.

"One of you has to die."

"Why? Why not get the information from us and then let us go?"

"Because as you said, you have half the information and he has the other half. Neither of you can go after the treasure with only half the information. Whoever has all the info gets the treasure, and I have to be assured that no one else has all of the map. If I let you both go, you'll tell each other your half of the secret to head me off."

I swallow hard and pull my head from his touch as anger pulses through me. I try to come up with a new plan to escape, but nothing comes to me immediately. All I can think is that the drugs they've pumped Langston with will wear off soon, and then he'll find a way to escape. Maybe Enzo or Kai are on their way here to save us—or at least, save Langston. Hopefully, because I have no idea how to get both of us out of here alive.

"Who will live and who will die? You or Langston? I'll give you some time to decide, Miss Dunn. "

He walks out the first door and locks me in. I run to the door and attempt to throw it open, but the door won't budge. I run to the second, but the handle barely rattles.

I slump to the floor with tears in my eyes. Only one of us is going to survive this—and I already know what my decision will be.

19

LANGSTON

Why is Liesel trying to protect me? That's my job.

I've threatened her life.

Killed her fiancé.

Gotten married despite telling her I never would.

I've been awful to her. And yet, she still protects me. I won't let her. It's my job to defend her.

"No, Liesel," I plead for her not to do this, not to offer up herself to protect me in any way. I want to call her huntress, but I dare not use my nickname for her in the presence of these horrible men.

She doesn't even hesitate as she walks out of the room. It's almost as if she doesn't even hear me.

The door is shut after she leaves. A roar of pain rips through my body, but because of my drugged up state, it doesn't leave my stomach. My head spins with a fog, and my body doesn't function. I try to tell my legs to move, to stand up, but the signal gets lost between my brain and my legs. My muscles feel like jello.

I fall forward, trying to go after her.

"Easy there, don't injure yourself on our watch. We'll

have our asses ripped if there is a single new mark on you," one of the guards left in my room says.

"Just wait until the drugs have worn off; you two will be the first to die," I threaten.

The man chuckles. "Who says we are ever going to let the drugs wear off? We know what you are capable of, which is why we have to keep drugging you. We aren't stupid enough to let that happen."

They plan on keeping me drugged.

Shit.

I'm not going to be able to rescue Liesel. I'm going to have to find a way to fight through the drugs. I can do this; I just need time.

Move, leg.

It moves. Not enough to get me very far or to fight, but enough to give me hope that with enough practice, I'll be able to fight through the drugs I'm given. If I can pretend I'm still under the influence for longer and longer periods of times when I'm not, maybe I'll regain enough strength to get Liesel out of here.

"Don't wiggle off," one of the men says as he hooks his arm underneath one of my shoulders. The other man does the same to my other arm, and I'm dragged to a chair. It's more comfortable than the floor but doesn't make it any easier for me to escape.

What is Liesel going through?

Is she being tortured?

Beaten?

Raped?

Is she going to survive this, both physically and mentally?

Liesel Dunn is the strongest woman I know, but strength has its limits. At some point, she'll break and won't be able to heal.

The time ticks by slowly, so slowly I'm not sure if time

even exists. My body doesn't regain much strength as the minutes pass. I'm still as out of it as I was when I was first brought to this room.

My two guards spend their time smoking a cigar and drinking whiskey. They don't talk or provide me any entertainment, which only makes the time tick by slower.

I hear footsteps, and my heart begs for it to be Liesel. Not because her returning to this room would make her safer, but because I'm desperate to see her.

The door opens, and the suited man steps in. It's easy to tell he's in charge by what he wears and how he carries himself, with complete confidence and fearlessness. My two guards act like if they put one foot out of place, they will be castrated.

The man grins at me as he walks into the room. "I'm happy to see you're still in one piece."

I frown. "And I'm unhappy to see that you still are."

"Miss Dunn did put up quite a fight, but in the end, she relented."

I growl and try to jump from my chair, but my body doesn't function very well yet. The two men grab my shoulders and yank me back in my seat easily.

The man in the suit laughs, amused by my distress. He walks over to the small bar and pours himself a drink before taking the seat opposite me.

"Who are you?" I ask.

"Does it matter?" The slick man raises his eyebrows.

"No, I'll kill you all the same."

"I have no doubt that you'll try, and if I falter in any way, you'll succeed."

"Then why don't you seem more afraid?"

"Because as long as I have Miss Dunn in my possession, I have complete control over you."

I growl again. He's right, but I hate that he already knows my weakness.

"What did you do to Liesel? If you hurt one hair on her head, I'll torture you for years and only let you die once I've broken every bone in your body."

He smirks. "Liesel is still in one piece, don't worry. She's currently contemplating my proposition."

I hold my breath, terrified she'll offer her body in exchange for keeping me safe—something I couldn't live with. But from his smug expression, I'm afraid he's already touched her.

I scan his suit, looking for any signs he's hurt her. Claw marks, a ripped hole or pulling of fabric, anything from her struggle, but I don't see anything out of place on him. That reassures me slightly, but maybe it's my imagination and hope convincing me. He could have changed suits after he beat her, or he could have had another man attack her.

"What proposition?"

"As I'm sure you've guessed, I seek the treasure that only you and Liesel protect."

I nod. Of course, he's after the treasure. I can't think of any other reason why he would capture both Liesel and me.

"For yourself or for your boss?" I ask. He may not tell me, but maybe he'll give me a clue as to a man higher up than him coming after us.

"Your questions don't stop, do they?" He takes a slow sip of his drink. "You won't get any answers, Mr. Pearce."

"Don't worry, I don't need to ask any more questions. Only a man who has vowed his life to another doesn't answer questions when asked. You are just like the men to either side of me. You're a low-life in a fancy suit, and you'll never have any real power."

He frowns, and I know I've hit a nerve.

"As I was saying, I gave Miss Dunn a proposition, and I've

decided to offer you the same deal. I can only make the deal with one of you, but again, it doesn't matter to me who it is."

I hold my breath. I don't care what the deal is; all I want is Liesel to be safe. I want to get on my knees and beg to keep him from hurting her. I would offer all the money I have to keep her safe. I'll give him the treasure, anything if he lets Liesel go.

"What's the deal?"

"You both tell me everything you know about the treasure. How to get it and what exactly it is."

"And in exchange?"

A Cheshire Cat smile spreads across his face while my heart thumps wildly in my chest. What will I have to give in order for Liesel to go free?

"And in exchange, I'll let one of you go free."

"Liesel will go free."

"You haven't heard the second half of my deal, so you might want to reconsider your chivalry."

I frown and hold my breath, waiting for him to drop the part he thinks will make me change my mind. He doesn't realize that nothing will make me change my mind. Liesel has to go free. I can't be responsible for her pain again, not when I have the chance to save her.

He takes another long drink, enjoying making me crazy as he draws this out.

"I'll let one of you go free—"

"Unharmed," I say.

He shrugs. "The person who goes free will be in one piece."

"They will be unharmed."

"You aren't in a position to negotiate. As I said, I gave Miss Dunn the same deal, and if she agrees to my terms before you do, then you will have no choice but to go along with it."

I frown.

"As I was saying before you rudely interrupted me, I will let one of you go free after I get the information I need. I'll kill the other one."

The blood drains from my face. "Why? Why not torture the other to within an inch of their life and then let them go?"

"I can't have the two of you exchanging information and fighting me for the treasure. I must be the only person who knows all of the clues."

I don't think I've blinked, taken a breath, or let my heart beat since he said he'd only let one of us live. I've been in predicaments like this before, life and death situations. Every time I've defeated the enemy. I've not only won but succeeded in killing the monster who dared to stand against me. I could do the same again.

But I've never been drugged like this and never had to keep Liesel safe at the same time.

If I choose Liesel to be the one to live, I won't be able to fight back until I know she's safe. By then, I could be dead. And I'm not sure I'm strong enough to fight the drugs. I don't know where Enzo and his team are, but my only hope is that they are close.

I'm made several vows in my life—to Phoenix, to my kids, to Liesel. I'm afraid I won't be able to keep all of them. I'll have to choose which vows to keep and which to break.

The man in the suit grins as he watches my agony. He's a sick, sadistic man who probably enjoys this as much as he will getting the information he needs to go after the treasure. The man finishes his drink casually, then stands and sets the glass back on the bar.

"Watch him, but don't injure him. Give him a half dose in a half-hour. I want him lucid when I return," he says to the two guards.

"Yes, sir," they both answer.

He looks at me. "I'll return in an hour to get your decision." He starts to walk to the door, and my heart speeds. *What if Liesel gives him an answer before me? Can I really let her decide both our fates?*

"Wait!" I shout as he opens the door.

He turns and looks at me with raised brows.

"You don't need to wait an hour. I have an answer for you now."

He smiles, satisfied.

"I'm sure you do, but I have a lunch meeting I need to attend, and I'll enjoy watching you squirm. You can give me your answer in an hour."

"What about Liesel?"

"I'll collect her answer in two hours if you don't give me an answer in one."

Then he leaves without giving me a chance to say more. He leaves me with my choice—an impossible one, but one I won't regret making. Not this time.

20

LIESEL

TIME CREEPS by until the man in the suit returns. I spend the entire time trying to break open the doors, but they're too thick. All I ended up doing was bruise my shoulder and hip.

I startle, stepping back when the suit opens the door.

"I know you may find my capabilities lacking, but I assure you, there is no escape from this castle unless I give permission for you to leave."

I shrug. "Do you blame a girl, destined to die, for trying?"

"No, I just thought you were smarter than that. I thought you knew not to waste your strength on a doomed task."

He shuts the door behind him, and I hear the faint lock as he does. We are locked in this room together.

"Would you like a drink?" he asks as he walks over to the bar in the corner of the room.

I've already raided it looking for water, food, anything alcohol-free to give me strength, but there is nothing but whiskey, vodka, and gin.

"No, thanks."

"Suit yourself." He pours himself a vodka and then sits on the couch.

I take a seat next to him, not because I want to, but because I need to preserve what little strength I have left. I feel practically naked sitting next to him, still only wearing Langston's leather jacket and black panties.

Did he have cameras watching what Langston and I did in the tower?

When he brought me up here before and bruised my ribs, did he touch me?

"What are you thinking about, beautiful?"

"Why did you call me beautiful?"

Goosebumps pour over my arms, uneasiness rocking my body.

He grins. "To make you uncomfortable."

"Are you always so honest?"

"I don't find any reason to lie."

"What is your name?"

"That's the question you want to ask me?"

"I'm tired of calling you 'the suit' in my head," I reply.

"You could call me, sir."

I frown. *No way in hell am I going to call him that.*

"Rowan Wells."

"I've made my decision, Rowan."

He smiles. "I knew you wouldn't give me the respect to call me, Mr. Wells."

"Why would I? You drugged me and my friend, then threw us in a tower with no way of escape, and now are threatening to kill one of us. I don't think you've earned my respect."

"Touché."

I take a deep breath, before telling Rowan my decision. "Langston must live. I choose him."

Rowan raises his eyebrows. "You'll choose death in order to save him?"

"Yes, kill me. Do whatever you want with me, just ensure that Langston lives."

"I didn't know that such love could exist, but I was wrong."

I'm about to open my mouth to say I don't love Langston, and I have no doubt that he doesn't love me, but what's the use? It doesn't matter why I'm saving him, just that Rowan accepts my deal.

"Do we have a deal? I'll answer any questions you have, and you can ask Langston any questions you have of him. And after we are finished, you will let Langston go free."

He holds out his hand to me, and I reluctantly take it, revolting from his frosty touch. "We have a deal, Miss Dunn."

We shake, and I'm careful not to be the first to pull away. I don't want to show any weakness, even though my lack of food and water is beginning to get to me. My head is spinning, my sight is fuzzy, and my body feels lethargic.

"What now?" I ask.

"Now, we chat. After we are finished, I'll have a chat with Langston. And then I'll set him free, far away from here, so he doesn't attempt a rescue."

"Where do you want me to start?"

"By telling me what is on your half of the letter your father gave you."

I frown. "How do you know about the letter? And that it was split between the two of us?"

He shakes his head. "I'm the one asking the questions, Miss Dunn, not you. What did the letter say?"

I consider my options. I have to tell him some truths, but I don't intend to tell him everything. He'll believe what I have to say. Langston will be safe whether I tell the full truth or not.

"The letter said that there was a treasure that would change my life. It didn't specify what the treasure was, just that it exists. The letter told me not to search for it, that it could destroy me."

"Get to the specifics, Miss Dunn; stop stalling."

I roll my eyes. "I'm just telling you what the letter said. The letter also said that whoever goes after it has to be married. They need to be madly in love in order to seek the treasure." I leave out that only a Dunn is able to get the treasure. I don't want him changing his mind and deciding to keep me alive.

He frowns, and I look down at his bare ring finger.

"I take it you're not married?" I smirk.

"I'm not."

"Well, you better find a wife quick if you want to go after the treasure."

He stares at me like I could be that wife.

"You want me dead, remember? I can't be your wife."

He growls. "Continue."

"The letter says you can only find the treasure where the sea takes you."

"What does that mean?"

I shrug. "There is a reason I haven't figured out where the treasure is; I only have half the information."

"Why, if you care so dearly about Langston and vice versa, haven't you both shared all the information with each other?"

Because he's wrong about us. We don't actually care about each other.

"For the same reason you won't let us both live. Us both only having a piece of the puzzle has ensured our survival to this point."

He nods and then leans back on the couch, waiting slightly more patiently for me to continue. He almost looks bored with my tale.

"There was something about meeting a man in Egypt

where he's hidden a clue. A partial password 862. And to follow the stars if you ever get lost."

Rowan looks at me suspiciously. "Was there anything else in your half of the letter?"

"No," I lie. Most of what I gave him was a lie, but it all rattled off my tongue with confidence. There is no way to tell if I made everything up or told the truth. That is until he speaks to Langston and none of my information fits with his.

"I'll go speak with Langston and then be back shortly," Rowan says, standing.

"How will you get him to speak to you?" I'm afraid he's planning on torturing him to get him to speak.

He grins at me. "By making the same deal with him."

"What?" I breathe.

"I'm sure he'll spill his guts to save you. Although, I suspect he'll be more truthful."

He stands and heads to the door, but I can't let him leave, not until I'm assured that he won't hurt or kill Langston.

I jump up, suddenly full of strength, and run to him.

"You made a deal with me! You can't hurt Langston." I grab his arm, trying to get him to stay and talk to me.

"You lied to me, Miss Dunn."

"I didn't," I plead.

"I don't believe you."

"Don't hurt him. You promised to let him go. Please."

He shakes his head. "I'll do what is necessary to get the information I seek."

I don't know what his words mean. *Have I been a fool for trusting him? Should I have told him the entire truth? Would that have ensured Langston survived, or was his plan all along to kill us both?*

"Don't worry, I still plan on keeping one of you alive; I just haven't decided who yet."

"Him—keep Langston alive."

"Maybe you should have told me the truth, and I would consider your plea."

He goes to open the door, and I grip his arm, trying to keep him with me. If he's with me, he can't hurt Langston.

"Let go," he orders.

"Promise me you won't hurt him, and I'll tell you the truth."

He pauses, as if considering my deal, but then I see his fist coming at my face.

I try to turn, but the impact hits me all the same. He knocks me hard in the jaw, forcing my feeble body to fall back to the floor.

Before I know what's going on, Rowan is gone. My tears fall immediately—not from my own pain, but from the fear of losing Langston. I failed in saving him, and I don't know what to do to fix it.

21

LANGSTON

"Is that everything?" he asks me, sitting in his suit like this is a business arrangement, and not like I've been drugged and tied up like an animal. I was only given a half dose this last time, so I don't feel as out of it as I did before, but that's why he added chains to my arms and legs.

I sit quietly, trying to remember anything else I can about my half of the letter.

"I believe so."

He nods. I'm not sure if this man believes me or not, but I've told him everything. Every word I said was the truth.

"Thank you for your honesty, Mr. Pearce."

I exhale an exhausted breath. I would do anything to save Liesel. Even if it makes me a terrible father, I've failed so many times to protect Liesel before.

I still have hope I'll be able to escape once Liesel is safely away, but if I can't, I know my kids will understand why I made this sacrifice. Enzo, Zeke, and Beckett will step in and make excellent father figures in my place. My children won't grow up without a father or with an evil one. Me staying alive isn't a requirement for them to grow up safely.

"You believe me?"

"I do."

"What happens next? Where will you set Liesel free?"

His eyes cut to me, and from the look in them, I've been lied to.

"Where. Are. You. Releasing. Liesel?"

He stands up.

I try to tackle him, but my restraints keep me in my chair.

"I wish I could say I'm a man of my word, but I'm not. You should have expected as much."

"Release her. I'll help you get the treasure. I'll do anything you want. Release her!"

He smirks. "Liesel made me a better offer."

My heart sinks. He's going to rape her, do unthinkable things to her body before he kills her. I can see it in the gleam in his eyes.

"Please," I beg.

"You two are the strangest couple I've ever met. I don't know how you can be married to another woman, when you so clearly love her."

I don't love her. I don't correct him; it's not worth the energy.

"Let her go."

He shakes his head. "I will keep my word to her. I'll let you go. Enjoy your freedom, Mr. Pearce. But know that she'll be dead long before you can save her. And if you return, I'll have no choice but to kill you, too. So for the sake of your children, I suggest you get on with your life and forget about her."

Forget about Liesel? Impossible.

The nameless man walks out the door, and I strain against my metal chains with everything inside of me.

"Hold still, and we'll get you out of here, man," one of the guards says, grabbing onto the restraints on my arms.

I continue to thrash like a great white shark on dry land. I have to escape. I have to get to Liesel.

"Sedate him," the head guard says to the other. "We can dump him far away from here, and we won't have to deal with him."

"But then he'll be dead weight, and I don't want to carry him."

I throw an elbow in one of the men's faces, hitting him in the nose and gushing blood.

"I'll do it. I don't want a broken nose like you," he chuckles to himself as he goes to grab another syringe.

No! If they sedate me, I won't be able to fight. I'll never be able to live with myself if they hurt Liesel.

I have to find a way to keep the drug from entering my system. My blood is boiling with rage and adrenaline by the time the squat, balding man returns. The other man's nose is still bleeding.

"I'm going to get some ice for my nose while the drug takes effect, then we can deal with him," the first guard says before walking out the door.

The man with the syringe approaches me from the back. I have to come up with a plan, something to stop the drug from taking over.

I continue to thrash as the man tries to grab ahold of me.

"Hold still," he says.

I don't. I jerk wildly as I feel him jab my shoulder. I feel him start to push the liquid into my muscle, and I pull away as he pushes in the liquid.

"There. Now you'll relax," the man says as he walks out of the room, leaving me tied to the chair.

I don't know if he pushed all of the drug into my shoulder or if I succeeded in spilling most down my back. I feel a coolness on my spine, and I hope it's some of the spilled liquid, but it's probably wishful thinking.

My eyelids grow heavy, confirming that at least some of the drug entered my system. I just hope it doesn't last. I hope that I can regain my strength before they move me from this castle. For now, I have to sleep.

No, I have to stay awake. I have to fight.

Think about Liesel. Think about what she could be going through. Think about her dead.

I feel sleepy and tired, but the pull of the drug never fully pulls me under.

When I hear footsteps approaching again, I pretend I'm asleep, so they think the drug worked. I force myself to slump in my chair, my eyes to close, and my breathing to still.

"He seems out," one of the men says.

I feel a finger poking me. I moan softly, but otherwise, don't move.

"Yep, looks good to go."

I hear and feel the unlocking of my chains. I want to make a run for it, but I have to be patient. I have to choose the exact right moment.

"Should we remove the restraints? He weighs a ton by himself; I don't want to have to carry anything I don't have to."

"We can remove the chains from his legs, but keep his wrists cuffed together in case he wakes up earlier than we expect."

I feel the chains being removed from my legs and my heart rate speeds. Luckily, these idiots don't notice the change in my pulse.

"I'll take his shoulders; you carry his legs."

"Which way are we taking him?"

"We'll take him out the back door and then pull the truck around to toss him in the back. Then drive him to the boat and dump him on the mainland somewhere."

I decide to wait until they carry me out of the house before I make my move. They will be exhausted from carrying me, and if I'm lucky, they will leave me alone while they get the truck. I just have to stay conscious until then, a slightly more difficult task while keeping my eyes closed. My body wants to fall asleep, while my heart and soul want to fight.

They lift me clumsily in the air, practically dragging me against the floor. I suspect I'll hit several bumps in the floor while they carry me and will have to force myself to not react.

My intuition proves correct.

My back is scraped all up and down from hitting the jagged stone floor. My shoulder feels ablaze from being dragged by the arms, but I never react.

Finally, I'm dropped onto softer ground. I hear a bird chirping, feel the warmth of the sun, and smell fresh-cut grass.

"I'll pull the truck around; you watch him."

I hear footsteps crunching on leaves as the guard walks away.

I wait a second longer, and then I attack. I stand and run at the remaining man. I wrap my chains around his neck and begin to choke him before he even realizes I'm awake. Within seconds, I drain the life from him, and he drops to the ground.

I find his gun and wait around the corner for his friend to return. When I spot him driving the truck up, I take aim and kill him with a single shot.

I don't know if there are cameras or other guards nearby who could be alerted, but I don't stick around to find out. I have one mission—find Liesel and get us both out of here.

The door that leads back to the house is unlocked, so I easily slip back inside. My wrists are still bound together, but there is enough space between them for me to use the gun without any trouble. But if a fight gets into hand to hand combat, I'm not sure how I'd fare with the chains and my drowsiness. My goal is to shoot any guards dead before a fight gets that far.

I don't know where Liesel is being kept. I don't know her condition or if everything the man in the suit said was a lie. I just know I have to get to her.

I come to a fork, where the hallway splits. The room I was kept in is on the right. I know instinctually to head to the left. Our captor would keep us at either ends of the castle to make it as hard as possible for us to reach each other.

There are several doors through the hallway. I want to burst through them all to see if Liesel is in each and every one of them, but I don't know who is on the other side of the door, and I won't risk getting captured again.

Instead, I'm stealth-like as I approach each door quickly but carefully. I place my ear against the thick doors. They may be thick, but they aren't modern. Thankfully, I can hear beyond the door into each room.

Two men are talking behind the first door, but neither of them mention Liesel after a few seconds.

I move on to the second door, and hear nothing—empty.

Finally, I make it to the third door where I hear sobs that wrap around my heart like prickly vines. Liesel is crying, and it breaks me.

I hold the gun carefully in my hand in case she's in the middle of being tortured. I'll kill every motherfucker who dares to touch her.

I pop the door open and aim around the room, expecting to take out the devil and his minions. Instead, all I see is Liesel.

I drop to my knees next to her. She hasn't looked up yet to realize that it's me.

"Please," she begs.

"Huntress," I say as soothingly as I can.

She lifts her head.

I gasp and immediately wish I could take my reaction back. But her face startles me—it's black, blue, and swollen. I don't know the extent of the rest of her injuries, but my imagination runs wild with horrid images of what the man in the suit did to her.

"Are you really here?" she whispers through her tears.

"Yes, I'm here."

She smiles as she falls against my chest. "You're here to save me?"

I nod with her head under the crook of my chin. My arms are useless to hold her like I want between how injured they are, the chains, and the gun I'm still gripping.

She thinks I'm her savior.

I will do whatever it takes to get her out of this castle, but I'm not her savior. I always fail at rescuing her until it's too late. This time is no different.

"You shouldn't have saved me," she whispers.

2 2

LIESEL

You shouldn't have saved me.

Those words ring truer than any I've ever spoken. My head rests against his chest for a split second, but I'm terrified that Rowan or one of the guards is going to come back and kill Langston on the spot.

"We have to go," Langston says, ignoring my comment.

"Is there anything I can do about the chains?"

"No."

"Do you have a gun or weapon for me?"

"No, and even if I did, you wouldn't aim to kill."

He's right, but I could still do some damage.

He stares at me like something's wrong with me. "Do you want me to carry you?"

"Could you?" I raise an eyebrow.

"Yes," he growls.

"No, I don't need you to carry me."

He starts to walk toward the door he entered through, but I grab his hand, stopping him.

"This way," I nod in the direction of the other door. "It leads straight outside the castle."

He walks in front of me. "Stay behind me, Liesel. Do not jump in front of me, understand? Don't you dare try to take a bullet for me."

"Lead the way," is all I say. I won't make any promises.

He sighs and then pushes the door open as I grab onto his hips and duck down as we walk through the door, short hallway, and then out the front door.

"Where are all the guards?" I whisper.

"I killed a couple of them, but I'm not going to wait around to find the rest. Want to run through the forest or steal a car?"

Before I can answer, we hear voices approaching.

"Woods," I mouth at him.

He nods, and he backs me into the brush while he keeps his gun aimed in the direction of the castle, until we get to the thick of the forest where we can no longer be seen. Then, we start running.

Langston isn't as fast as me, I realize, which makes me try to study him as we run.

"Are you hurt?" I ask.

"Drugged."

I frown. "Are you going to pass out on me?"

"No, I only got a partial dose. I'll be fine soon, but it's best to keep my adrenaline up to help get the drug out of my system faster."

I nod, and we keep running. It's a bit freeing to be running through the woods with my childhood friend. Even though I'm barefoot and pantless, and we are running for our lives, it's still enjoyable. This is what I missed the most about Langston, being together like this.

He must feel it too, because he gives me a knowing smile before turning back around.

Suddenly, his smile drops, as do his feet. I stop and turn when I see what we are running toward—the edge of a cliff.

"What do we do?" I ask as we both look over the edge.

"We have two choices—run along the perimeter of the island and try to find a boat, or we jump."

"Jump? And where would we swim to?"

"Do you see that land?"

I nod.

"It looks like it's only a few miles from here."

I nod, understanding. It's an exhausting swim. I turn and look back. I won't go back to the castle, and I won't allow Langston to die at Rowan's command. We could circle the island, but it only gives the men more opportunity to find us. They won't suspect that we jumped into the water. And since no boats are missing, it will take longer for them to search for us across the channel.

Then I look at his hands. "You aren't going to be able to swim with those chains."

We both look over the edge, searching for options. There's some driftwood floating nearby.

"I have to try."

Langston has always been a fish in water. He's always belonged in the ocean. And I know if he were to die, he'd prefer the ocean swept him away.

"On the count of three," I say to gather strength.

"One," he says.

"Two," I say.

"Three," we both say as we leap.

I don't know how tall the cliff is, but the fall seems to go on forever. We hit the water, and I immediately start kicking as hard as I can toward the surface. I'm not afraid that I won't take another breath, but I need to make sure Langston makes it to the surface.

I breach the surface at the same time Langston does. We both smile wide.

"Here," Langston pushes a piece of wood in my direction.

I grab onto it, and then he grabs hold of another. We both turn ourselves in the direction of the closest piece of land and start kicking.

I don't think I breathe until we are at least halfway between the island and the far shore.

"Do we know what country we are in?" I ask as we swim.

"No, I didn't get much information out of the suit."

"The suit?"

"The man in charge."

"Oh, you mean Rowan Wells."

"He told you his name?"

"I demanded he tell me, and he did."

His eyes widen. "You are a better manipulator than I thought."

"I'll take that as a compliment."

Our kicking continues to get slower the longer we go. The water gets cooler as the sun begins to set. I don't know what I'm more afraid of—freezing to death in this water or drowning from exhaustion.

"Do you think there are sharks in this water?" I ask, trying to distract us with a different type of gloom.

"I'm sure there are."

I shiver, and he laughs at me.

"Don't tell me my kick-ass, warrior in a dress and heels, survived torture, huntress is afraid of sharks?"

"Everyone is afraid of sharks. Haven't you watched any horror movies? Sharks are one of the top killers."

He laughs, which makes me smile. I'm shocked I can still make him laugh.

"So, what's the plan when we make it to shore?" I ask.

"Find some shelter, ideally some food and warm clothes, and pray we find someone who will let us use a phone, computer, or something to contact Kai and Enzo without drawing too much attention to ourselves. Then we hide and hope Kai and Enzo find us before Rowan does."

I look out at how far we have left to go. I'm beginning to doubt I have the strength. "And if we're too tired to make it to shore tonight?"

"Don't talk like that. We're strong enough. Trust me, I won't let us drown."

"Then, start talking. I'm going to need a lot of distraction if I'm going to make it to shore without whining the whole way."

"I can provide a distraction," he flashes me a wicked grin with a wink, and I know his mind has gone to very dirty places.

I think I'm going to enjoy the rest of our swim.

23
LANGSTON

I MADE A MISTAKE. I should have insisted that we found a boat to take us across instead of swimming this length. We've been swimming half the day, and we still have a long way to go.

We are both exhausted and freezing.

Liesel is a trooper. She's barely complained, has been kicking harder than I have, and is usually further ahead of me in the ocean.

But from how my own body aches, I know she's struggling. And I know how much she hates the ocean—this is her own special kind of torture.

The drugs in my system finally wore off an hour ago, which only left a massive headache in their place. I'm dehydrated and my legs are cramping, but that's nothing compared to the burning fire in my shoulder as I grip the driftwood. I really need to have a doctor look at my shoulder. I suspect that I'm going to need surgery and rehab to every use it again without pain, but that will have to wait.

It would be easier to stop and let the ocean take me, but

there is no way I'm giving up—not on Liesel and not on my kids.

I try to think of something funny to distract us, but I can't come up with anything. I want to ask her about what happened back in the castle. *How did she get the suit to tell him his name? What deal did she make with him? Why did she make the deal?*

But conversations like that need to wait until we are on shore and face to face.

"What are you thinking about? Because the look on your face says you're undressing me with your eyes and thinking of dirty, filthy things you want to do to me," Liesel says.

I grin, glad to hear her interpretation. *She wants me dirty? I can be dirty.*

"Just trying to decide if I'd rather fuck you in the ocean or on the sand. Which would be hotter?"

She scrunches her nose. "Neither."

I laugh. "Because I disgust you?"

"No, I have no problem fucking a good looking man if there is little chance we are going to survive tomorrow. But the ocean is freezing, and the sand is messy."

"Would you consider the ocean if I warmed you up?"

"Maybe," she says.

"Or the sand if I promised you could be on top and I'd clean you off afterward?"

"Hmm," she purrs.

I grin but don't get too excited. We're just blabbing to distract ourselves. We aren't fucking—now or ever.

We don't talk for a while. We just focus on kicking and keeping our heads above water. The sun begins to set, and the cool water turns ice cold. Every part of me is numb. My head falls onto the driftwood, too hard to hold up. I can no longer see where we are going.

"Langston," Liesel whispers.

My eyes flutter open, and I realize I've practically been asleep while kicking.

"Look!"

I lift my head, taking almost all the strength I have left. But it's worth the effort—shore.

"We're going to make it," we both say at the same time with a renewed energy.

We kick harder, and luckily, the tide gives us a push as well until our feet hit sand. We stumble up to get out of the water, and then we crash onto the sandy beach, collapsing with heavy breaths.

"We made it. I can't believe we just did that," Liesel says.

I nod. I don't want her to think we are out of danger, but I don't want to worry her either. We both need to rest before we move on. We just can't rest as long as we need, or it will all be for nothing.

The moon is shining down on us, and for once, I think we finally did something right.

"We should get up and find a better place to rest for tonight," I say.

"Okay."

Liesel pushes herself up and then holds out her hand to me. I don't want to seem weak, but she's the physically stronger between the two of us right now. I take her hand, and she helps me up.

"Can you walk?" she asks, still gripping my hand.

I look down at where our hands meet. "I can with you by my side."

"Good, then let's go."

We start walking up the beach and into the nearby forest. I don't know where we are in the world, and I don't care. We just need to find some shelter for tonight and hope that Rowan doesn't find us. In the morning, it will be easier for us to escape once we've regained our strength.

"What are we looking for?" Liesel asks.

I stop suddenly. "That—that is what we are looking for."

A small cabin sits in the woods. There are no cars parked in the gravel drive and no lights on.

I pull my gun from where I fastened it to my waistband.

"You're not going to shoot an innocent person," Liesel commands.

"I'm not, but it could be a trap. Or if someone does live here, they might try to protect their property if they see me. I won't hurt them unless they work for Rowan."

"Okay," she says.

"Stay here, and let me check it out."

I know she wants to protest, but she stays put as I circle the cabin. It looks like someone's summer cabin, but from the chill in the air, it's no longer summer here. I peer in through several windows, and after not seeing any sign of anyone, I circle to the backdoor and kick it open.

I search through the dark but don't find any signs of people currently living here. I walk to the front and open the door.

"It's clear. Come in," I say.

Liesel walks inside the cabin, and I shut the door behind her. The lights are still off, but I can tell she's shivering. I want nothing more than to put my arms around her. The only problem is my hands are still cuffed.

"Is it safe to turn the lights on?" Liesel asks.

I nod. It would be best to keep the lights off, but right now, we need simple comforts like electricity.

Liesel finds the light switch, and the lights turn on, illuminating us both.

I look at Liesel. She's drenched; goosebumps stand out through the sand and mud stuck to her legs. The leather jacket she kept on to keep her warm is dripping water everywhere, and her hair is a matted mess of water and seaweed.

She looks at me the same way, with disgusted disbelief. I'm just as soaked. My jeans are stuck to me, and the handcuffs dug ugly red marks around my wrists.

"We need to figure out a way to get those cuffs off you; then we can figure out the rest."

"Let's look for something to pick the lock." I saw an ax to chop firewood in front of the shed out back, but I'd prefer to have the cuffs off, not just separated.

Liesel starts to head toward one of the bedrooms to look.

"Stay," I say, unable to get my words out fast enough.

She turns and stares at me with her mouth open and eyes narrowed. "Why? I thought I was supposed to help you look for something to pick the lock with."

"Yes, but don't leave my sight. I don't want to worry about you, and I'm the only one with a weapon."

She keeps staring at me confusedly.

"Please," I add.

She returns to my side, and we head to the kitchen first.

I find a knife. She finds a paperclip.

I hand the knife to her. "Keep this with you at all times."

She takes it reluctantly, and I take the paperclip from her. It takes me a minute to get the first lock to come free on my left wrist, but then the second pops open easily, and the chains drop to the floor.

"Here," Liesel says, putting a cool dish rag over my wrists to soothe the pain.

"Thank you." I clear my throat. "You should shower and see if you can find any clothes to warm you up. I'll keep look out here and see if I can find any food for us."

She nods and then heads to the bathroom in back of the house; I follow at a distance to keep her somewhat near. I hate letting her out of my sight at all, but she needs to shower, and I will listen carefully for any intruders.

The fridge is practically empty besides some expired

ketchup and dressing bottles. The pantries have a few cans of beans and vegetables. I pull those out and find some frozen pizzas in the deep freezer.

I pop the pizzas in the oven just as Liesel comes back into the kitchen.

"That wasn't a very long shower," I say.

"I didn't want to be apart from you any longer than I had to."

I turn to look at her and grin.

"I like this look."

She holds out her arms, and a flannel shirt hangs down well past her hands. Black sweatpants start to drop from her hips, but she grabs them.

"It's all I could find. A man must live in this house alone. I can't wait to see you in flannel."

I want to kiss her, to hold her in my arms, but I'm still soaking wet and filthy. She's clean, and I don't want to ruin her new clothes.

"I put a couple of frozen pizzas in the oven, but there are a couple of cans of beans on the counter if you get hungry before they're done."

She nods and walks to the kitchen to peek in on the pizzas.

"Here." I hold out the gun to her. "Hold on to this until I get back from the shower."

She stares at it. "No, it's better off with you. I have my knife. If someone comes, you'll save me."

I frown, hating her comment, but knowing she's right. I go to the bathroom to shower and dress as quickly as possible. The task is hard because of how sore and dizzy I am, never mind that I can barely lift my right arm to shoulder height. But I make do and dress in a flannel shirt and khaki pants.

When I return to the kitchen and catch sight of Liesel

pulling the pizza out of the oven, my heart beats again.

She smiles at me as she places the pizzas on plates and then carries them to the small kitchen table where she's already filled two large glasses of water.

I try not to completely collapse into the chair as to not worry Liesel, but the sound the chairs makes when I sit gives me away. Liesel frowns, but we don't speak of it. We both dig into the food and drink every drop of water.

We both keep our eyes on each other as we eat, trying to find answers to all our burning questions without actually asking them. I need to ask her what happened. I need to find out how broken she is, how much she hates me for not rescuing her sooner. But I'm enjoying the way she's batting her eyelashes at me, the way her skin is glowing after her shower, and how adorable she looks in oversized flannel.

But I can't get past the bruises on her face, though. I certainly can't face what other bruises and marks I may be missing beneath the flannel.

"I'm sorry," I start after we both have enough food in our bellies to have this talk.

"What do you have to be sorry about?"

"I'm sorry that I couldn't save you. I got there too late." I think of Rowan's face, how smug he was that she'd made him a better offer. I close my eyes as I relive that memory. My mind goes to him beating her, raping her, taking everything left of her—all because I couldn't fight off two men, some chains, and a drug fast enough.

"Langston." I feel her hand on mine, and I open my eyes to find her kneeling in front of me.

"What are you doing?" I stand up abruptly and pull her up until she's standing too.

"I'm trying to break through your horrid imagination."

"What do you mean?"

She touches my hand to her face. "This is the worst that

happened to me. I wasn't beaten. I wasn't tortured. I wasn't raped."

My eyes dart side to side, trying to figure out if she's telling the truth or not. But all I find is an odd kindness staring back at me.

"You saved me before anything could happen."

"Thank god," I exhale sharply and painfully.

She shivers.

"Let's go sit on the couch. I'll start a fire, and we can tell each other everything that happened and make a plan to get out of here," I say.

She nods, and our hands interlock as I lead her to a spot on the couch. Luckily, there is already wood by the fireplace, so I don't have to go out into the cold so soon. I start the fire and then sit down next to Liesel.

"Tell me everything."

She stares at me with a blank expression. "I think you've pieced together most of it."

"You took a deal with Rowan?"

She nods.

"Who did you choose to go free?"

She lets go of my hand. "I chose you."

I frown. "And that would mean that he'd kill you?"

She nods.

"Why? Why would you save me when I've been nothing but horrible to you? I killed your fiancé and threatened to kill you! Your decision was easy; why would you save me?"

She bites her lip as she considers her next words. I think she's going to say something about not being able to take a father away from her kids. Or a joke answer about wanting to be the one to kill me myself. Or maybe she thought if I was free, I could come back and save her before Rowan killed her, which would have been risky.

"You would have never killed me," she says.

I frown, although, maybe she's right. Maybe I wouldn't have. I don't know.

"I couldn't choose my life over yours. And I know you made the same decision. You chose to keep me alive instead of saving yourself."

"Why?" I ask again, begging her to say the words I've wanted to hear her say since I was fifteen and first noticed her turning into a woman, no longer just my neighbor, closest friend, and later enemy. I've wanted her to say that we could be something more for so long.

She sighs as if she can't quite say the words she wants to say. Instead, she bemoans, "Why couldn't you have saved me before?"

That is what ultimately broke us—me not saving her. She can't forgive me for it, and I can't forgive myself.

Then, she leans forward, thrusting herself into my arms as she presses her lips against mine, expressing what she can't say with her kisses.

24

LIESEL

I DON'T KNOW why I kiss Langston. To keep myself from saying the words on the edge of my tongue. To keep from having to explain myself to him. Or just because I want something life-affirming after what we went through.

Whatever the reason, the kiss is exactly what we both need.

It fills my soul with warmth, kindness, and passion. His lips heat my body better than the fire ever could.

Langston tries to use his right arm to pull me closer, but he winces, forgetting how injured it is. He switches to his far less injured left hand to grab my hips. He's trying to move me closer to him, so I help him out by scooting my hips until I'm as close to I can be to him without climbing on top of him.

He pulls back. "Climb on my lap, huntress."

I can't deny either of us right now.

"Don't let me hurt you," I say as I straddle his lap.

He pushes my hips down, until I'm resting on top of him. "You could never hurt me."

Then he leans back on the couch, and my body falls on

top of his until my lips are once again pressed against his. My tongue pushes in his mouth this time, unable to resist tasting all of him.

Our moans echo through the room, tuning out the crackle of the fire.

Langston's hands rest at my hips and mine on his chest as we both enjoy each other's bodies. Each kiss pushes me closer to something I've wanted but denied myself for too long.

Closer.

Closer.

Closer.

Until I'm bursting with my decision. And yet, I still deny myself, deny us.

I lean back; I need to stop kissing Langston. I need to think straight before I make this decision.

"Is something wrong?"

Everything—everything is wrong.

I can't ask the question I really want. But sitting on Langston's lap, feeling the way I do, I feel like I don't need him to answer to know what I want—something I never thought I'd ever get.

"I choose you," I say.

Langston stares into my eyes, not understanding that I'm on the brink of a decision that will change both of our lives.

I always thought I hated Langston. I thought he hated me.

He chose to marry another. And I said yes to a fiancé.

We have both made threats and mistakes that have destroyed the other's life.

But none of that matters.

We could die tonight, tomorrow, next week, and all I can think is that I want Langston. I want him despite all the pain and heartbreak—whether it makes me a cheater and whore. No matter if I'm wrong and we are still enemies. If Langston still threatens my life after this night. If my heart completely breaks. Nothing will matter, because I will have had tonight.

"And I choose you," he says, before kissing my bottom lip tenderly, and falling back again with a sigh. He thinks our night is done and we should snuggle off together in bed. He doesn't know what I'm thinking. He doesn't realize that our words are as good as an 'I love you.'

"Fuck me, Langston."

His mouth falls open, just an inch, and his pupils dilate. "I don't think I heard you right."

"You did."

"Why…I mean, are you sure?"

"Yes, I've wanted you since I was sixteen. I never thought it would happen. The amount of hate, heartache, and pain we've caused each other almost ensured we never would, but if I'm going to die, I'd rather die knowing whether you are the worst or best fuck of my life."

He smiles. "Definitely the best. But I've got you beat; I wanted this since I was fifteen."

He grabs the back of my neck and pulls me to his lips, kissing me hard and hungrily on every spot of my lips as his tongue dances with mine. I'm so turned on from kissing him that I'm afraid I'm going to explode the second he enters me.

But then he pulls away, and I'm afraid he's changed his mind.

"Why are you frowning?" he asks, as he runs his thumb across my bottom lip.

"I'm afraid you're going to remember you're married, that you have a life waiting for you, that you hate me and are going to stop this."

He shakes his head. "My marriage means nothing, but if you need me to file for divorce, I will." He searches my eyes before continuing. "And I've never wanted anything more. I never thought you'd say yes, so I've never asked. But you don't ever have to doubt how much I want this. It probably won't change anything between us..." He kisses my ear, running his tongue lazily around it.

I shiver.

Then he continues. "But then again, it could change everything."

I catch my breath as his words put any doubt behind me. Things may end badly, I may become jealous or angry, but I won't regret this.

"Tonight, we are on the same side, huntress. I'm going to enjoy exploring every part of your body. I know we should sleep, but if these are to be my last hours, I can't imagine a better way to spend my time."

I suspect we've been on the same side more than just tonight, but I don't say that.

"Fuck me, killer. Make me forget every man before you, and spoil me for any man after."

When I say the word after, he growls possessively like he can't stand the thought of anyone after him.

I grin—that's up to him. Things won't change as much as Langston might like. Sex doesn't change much. We are still two broken people, hurt by the world, who, in return, have hurt each other to prevent ourselves from suffering further pain. We are still too controlling, too temperamental. If we tried to take a run at a real relationship, we'd spend the whole time fighting and bickering. Neither of us would survive, but we can survive one night of hot sex.

He stands with me in his arms.

"Langston!" I squeal. "Put me down; you don't want to hurt your arm."

He tilts his head, and then he buries his head against my neck. "I'd rather lose my arm than not fuck you properly. Don't worry about my arm; all I feel is you."

He starts walking, holding me as if he has the

strength of an ox, not like a man who has had his shoulder dislocated, was drugged, and then swam miles in open water while having his arms handcuffed together.

"And I want to fuck you in a proper bed for the first time. Then I plan on having you on every surface in this house," he growls.

He carries me effortlessly as his lips hungrily find mine. He doesn't flick the lights on as we enter the bedroom, which disappoints me. I need to see all of him when he fucks me.

"You have to stop pouting like that, huntress."

He winks at me as he lays me down on the bed. The room is pretty dark, so I can barely make out his shadow until a spark flickers. There's another fireplace in the bedroom, and now that he's started it, the room simmers with a romantic glow.

He moves around the room, lighting some candles on the nightstands to light the room enough where I can make Langston out clearly, but not so much that it ruins the effect. When he's finished, he walks back over to the bed and stands at the foot of the bed.

"You're going to have to trust me, huntress."

"What if I can't?"

"Then, I'll have to show you that you can."

He starts on the buttons of his flannel shirt, unbuttoning them slowly.

"My sexy lumberjack," I tease as I watch him strip at the foot of the bed.

He looks at me seriously, stone-faced. The tone shifts between us from playful to pensive.

He finishes the last button, removes his shirt and drops it on the floor. I've seen him shirtless plenty of times, we've lived together shirtless, but there's something different about seeing him this way and knowing what's going to come next.

I assume he's going to stop there and then work on undressing me, but he doesn't stop. He unbuttons his khaki pants and pushes them down his body, until he's standing naked in front of me.

My eyes immediately memorize everything about him. Every hard line, sharp edge, and roughness about his body. Every scar, mark, and bruise. My favorite part is the V that starts at his hip bones and guides my eyes to his long, thick, and veiny cock.

As soon as I see him standing naked before me while I'm still fully clothed, all my doubts vanish. My mouth waters, my eyes dilate, and my body tingles with anticipation.

He smiles softly at my reaction, knowing that such a small action gained a tiny bit of my trust. He didn't give me control, but he made himself vulnerable, which is a good start.

I tingle with anticipation and start unbuttoning my own shirt. He looks at me uncomfortably, holding back, but he lets me unbutton my own shirt. I need some control now in order to give up a little later, so he lets me have this moment.

The shirt falls open, and my bare breasts stare up at him. The bruise around my ribs has turned yellow and green and is barely visible beneath the glow of the fireplace, thank god.

His eyes grow, and his body tenses as he stares down at me. His hands are twitching to touch me, but he's letting me control this moment. I don't know how this is going to work between us—both battling to drive the sexual experience in the way we want.

I hook my thumbs into the waistband of my sweatpants and begin to move them down over my hips as I lay in front of Langston.

He bites his lips and fists his hands, rooting his feet into the ground to let me finish. But as I struggle to get the pants off my feet, he steps in.

He grabs my pants and yanks them off until I'm lying naked in front of him.

There's a part of me that wants him to become the alpha male inside him that he brings out when he's with other women. And then there's a part of me that wants his sweetness and obedience to my orders.

"Stop thinking so much," he whispers.

I rake my bottom lip through my teeth. "I'm trying, but I need you to promise me something first. Don't lie to me tonight. Not with your words and definitely not with your body. If there is one thing I need most of all, it's for us to be completely honest. If you hate fucking me, tell me."

He frowns. "First, it's not possible for me to hate fucking you. But I know what you mean—I won't lie, not to you, not now."

"I won't lie either."

He slowly inches himself over my body until his strong body is hovering over mine, not touching. I stare at his arms that must be aching.

"I won't lie, but I'm not going to be sweet and let you make the decisions. Your brain is on overdrive thinking too much right now." He takes my hand and kisses my palm. "Can you handle me taking control?"

A million sparks fly through my hand where he kisses me. "For now. I'll let you know when I want it back."

"You're something else."

"Kiss me," I say, bossing him around.

He leans down to kiss me but misses my lips purposefully and landing on the corner of my mouth.

I moan, needing him to kiss me properly. Needing him to press his body against mine. Needing so much and not sure if I'm going to get it tonight.

He takes his time kissing each corner of my mouth, then each side of my neck until I'm squirming beneath him. Only then does he kiss my lips. By then, any doubts or thoughts have disappeared.

His kisses are hungry and wild, not as controlled as I know he likes them to be—it seems he's letting go too.

Neither of us needs to be in control. We just need to let our bodies and souls take over.

Our eyes meet and seem to agree. His body presses down gently on top of mine. Our bodies fit perfectly, as if we were designed for each other.

His cock presses down on my lower stomach as his mouth reconnects with mine. His hand finds my breast as mine trails down his back. And then, as if we both decide at the exact same time, we flip. I'm on top; he's beneath me.

I claw at his chest and rub up against his cock, using him to get myself wetter before he enters me. His hands massage my breasts, flicking his thumbs across my sensitive nipples.

"You're drenched," Langston says with a smug smile.

I am—I'm so ready for him. I've been ready for him for years.

I lean down and kiss him as he bucks up against me.

Then, at the same time, we freeze.

"Condom?" I ask.

He frowns. "Any chance you think our cabin friend has one?"

I crawl up the bed, reluctantly letting go of Langston to dig into the drawer of the rugged-looking nightstand. I find cigarettes, a lighter, and a small bottle of rum, but no condoms.

I look around the room and see the door is open to the bathroom.

"Be right back," I run into the bathroom. I check every drawer and cabinet, but I find none.

I sigh, as I grip the counter.

"It's okay, I can just make you come," Langston says from the doorway. His eyes pour over me, drenching my pussy further. He looks at me like I'm the only woman in the world he's ever had eyes for.

"I could pull out?" he asks, as he steps behind me and wraps his arms around my waist.

I take a deep breath. I don't want to have our first and possibly only time together lack feeling him coming inside me.

I meet his eyes in the mirror. His eyes are soft, kind, and maybe even loving. Maybe I'm reading too much into his expression, but I know what I want.

"I trust you," I say.

He sucks in a breath when I touch his hand and slide his hand down my front so he can feel how wet I still am for him. Throughout my search, nothing changed; if anything, I want him more now than before.

"I'll pull—"

"No, I trust you. Take control. Fuck me like you want." If I get pregnant, we'll figure it out.

He fists my hair with one hand as he kisses me roughly down my neck and spine, while his other hand dips between my legs. He already knows how to work my body and clit, touching me with just enough pressure to make me weak in the knees.

"I've dreamed of this so many fucking nights...and as much as I would love to fuck you here and look into your eyes in the mirror as you come, I want you in a fucking bed our first time."

He flips me around until I fall into his body. I jump as he grabs my ass and hungrily kisses my body.

We walk into the bedroom and collapse on the bed

together—full of sweat, wetness, and saliva. All of it turns me on more.

He settles between my legs at the same time he lifts my hands and binds them together in his fist above my head. He doesn't push inside me; he lowers his head to bite my nipple with his teeth.

I expect there to be a nervous anxiety as he takes control of my body, but it never comes.

I trust him.

"Tell me you want me. Tell me how dirty your thoughts are. Tell me you want my cock." I see the tiniest hint of concern in his eyes, not sure if I'm going to back out. He really needs this, as much or more than me.

I slide my hips down, just enough to envelope the tip of his cock, but that's all the power he gives me. He slams inside me, filling me completely.

I gasp at how he fills me.

He stills as soon as he's fully inside me and our eyes lock once again. His fill with tears. He leans down and kisses me so tenderly on the lips. "Are you okay? I meant to be gentle, but I can't control myself with you."

"I'm more than okay."

"Good, because being inside you is fucking incredible."

Together we decide wordlessly when to start moving. My hips rock at the same time his begin to thrust, which makes us both smile. He's still gripping my hands above my head as he thrusts inside.

I've never felt anything like it—not with Waylon, not with any man. With Langston, I don't want to fight him. And even though he has absolute control over my body, I feel like I have all the power. If I move my hips, he moves his. If I slow my breath, he speeds up until I'm panting again.

"This—this is..." he can't finish his words as he slams into me.

I arch, driving him as deeply as I can into my body. We're both close to coming. We are close to ending this chapter. Seconds before we come, Langston releases my hands.

"I trust you, too."

One more thrust, and he's filling me with his warm cum and screaming my name, which pushes me into an explosion of an orgasm of my own.

"There was no way I would have killed you, not even if my life depended on it," Langston says, still inside me as he rolls himself onto his back and me on top. "I could never hurt you, huntress. All I've ever wanted to do was protect you from the demons, me included."

He would have never killed me. We said we would only tell truths tonight, and I believe him. He could never hurt me.

That also means that when he killed Waylon, he knew exactly what he was doing somehow. It's time to spill more of the truth, so he'll stop beating himself up. But for now, I want to fuck him until the sun rises.

25

LANGSTON

I HAVE to leave Liesel to get us some food. So far, I've done well on keeping my promise of fucking her on every surface in this small cabin. I've fucked her twice in the bed, once in the bathroom, and once on the couch. But unfortunately, we need more fuel if we are going to continue.

I feel the need to make up for a lifetime of not having her in one night. We have no idea what tomorrow brings. *Could Rowan's men be outside right now, ready to kill us? And if we survive, how do we deal with our pasts?*

I scrounge up some bottles of water and start digging through the cans to see which we should choose, when I feel Liesel's hands wrap around my naked waist, and her front rubs up against my back.

Jesus, one-touch and I'm already hard again. My shoulder is going to be sore tomorrow. I could possibly be doing permanent damage to the nerves in my arm, but I don't care. There isn't one thing about tonight that I'll regret.

"I missed you," Liesel says.

I moan as she finds my cock with her fingers and slides me through her fist.

"I've been gone for less than two minutes."

"It was too long," she says.

I groan, and I know the food is going to have to wait. There is someone I'd much rather eat. I let her thrust her hand over me one more time, ensuring I'm hard before I turn around.

She squeals when I slam her down on the counter, and part of the cabinet door falls open. It isn't the first piece of furniture I've broken tonight. The bedframe broke right down the middle I fucked her so hard.

I spread her legs wide and then sweep my fingers over her opening. She's wet. She's been wet for me all night. I've seen her fuck Waylon all night, but this feels different. With him, she required to be in control. She tied him up, bossed him around, forced him to wear a condom.

Tonight, we are both just going with the flow. Doing everything we've ever dreamed of doing. Living for all the years we might not.

The second I find her wet, I brace her legs as I push inside, slamming her hard against the cabinet. We both like wild, passionate sex. The kind that breaks things and pushes our limits. The kind where we battle with our tongues, our touch, our thrusts.

She grabs my hair and yanks hard as I pound into her again. She tilts my head and takes over my mouth while I grab harder onto her thighs.

I don't know how we fit so well together. I was always afraid sex with Liesel was going to be impossible because of the damage we come from. But somehow, our roughness and insecurities fit together. I push and she pulls. When she yanks, I jerk. Like magnets, that if pushed together the wrong way repel each other, when we turned the correct way, we are pulled together by forces greater than ourselves.

She bites my lip as I grab hold of her ass and deepen my thrusts.

She growls.

I moan.

Until tears threaten her eyes.

I hurt her—fuck.

But it's too late to stop now. Our orgasms are crashing down on us in waves. Another chance that I could get her pregnant. I never asked if she's on the pill or another form of birth control that might still have some effect now. I didn't ask what day she is in her cycle. But I suspect because of the conditions we've been held in, combined with stress and lack of food, it's very unlikely that I'll get her pregnant. Not that I wouldn't welcome another child, but I don't want to complicate an already complicated situation.

I grab onto her hips as I fill her with more of my seed, and I feel her orgasm squeeze around me. Only once our orgasms have passed can I finally wipe away her tear.

"I'm sorry, was I too rough?"

She smiles through her tears. "No, I'm sorry. I haven't cried in years. You opened the floodgates, and now I cry about everything."

"Are these happy tears?"

"They're everything tears."

I run my hand through her wavy, blonde locks, and then I kiss her forehead. I don't know how I ever thought I could kill her, no matter what she did. Liesel Dunn doesn't deserve to die, and no matter what nickname she uses, I'll never be her killer.

"Now, we really must eat or drink something or we'll pass out," I say.

She pouts.

I laugh and turn around. "Climb on."

She laughs as she climbs onto my back and wraps her

legs and arms around my naked body as I begin to open drawers to find a can opener.

"How are we going to get back tomorrow, do you think?" Liesel asks.

I haven't told her I found a satellite phone in one of the drawers. I'm not ready to be rescued yet. I'm afraid of what will happen when we return to the real world.

I finally got Liesel. I'm not ready to give her up. I don't know if I'll ever be.

"Together," I answer.

I don't know what will happen tomorrow, but we will arrive there together.

26

LIESEL

"ENZO IS COMING TO GET US," Langston says, waking me.

I pull the covers up to my chin but don't wake up fully. I'm too happy in the mattress, even though I only slept for probably less than an hour last night and Langston had to sleep directly on the floor since we broke the frame.

Langston walks over and sits on my edge of the bed.

I frown—he's put boxer briefs back on, which means he's not going to fuck me again.

"I have coffee," he says, holding a red camping mug out to me.

I sigh but sit up and take the mug from him.

He smiles softly at me as his eyes drag down from my matted hair to my naked torso.

"Wait…Enzo is coming?"

"Yes, I found a satellite phone when I was looking for the coffee beans. I let you sleep for as long as I could, but we need to leave in five to meet him in a nearby field."

I sip the bitter coffee. We're leaving. I should be happy we are getting rescued. Rowan and his men won't be able to kill us, but I'm not happy. I've never been more unhappy.

"What's wrong? Is the coffee bad?"

I nod. "It's a bit stale."

"You can sleep on the helicopter, and we can get more caffeine when we get back to Miami."

I give him a measured smile. "I better get dressed."

His eyes dart away to give me privacy as I head to the bathroom. I purposely don't close the door as I shower quickly, hoping that Langston will join me, but after spending all of my five minutes in the shower, I get dressed, disappointed and lonely.

It seems our one night together is over. Our connection is all in the past now. The sex, lust, passion is all gone.

I run my hand through my hair, as I can't find a comb, when Langston finally pops his head in. "Ready?"

I nod and follow him out of the house. We are both wearing our lumberjack outfits again, but I couldn't find any shoes that fit me. All I have on my feet are thick socks, unlike Langston, who found real shoes. He moves much faster through the thick brush than I can. I keep stepping on thorns, and my soreness and foul mood aren't helping.

"Hop on," Langston says, crouching down in front of me.

"I can walk."

"I know, but I'm tired of listening to your grumbling, and we'll get out of here and to safety much faster if you get on my back."

I jump on his back with a thud.

He grunts but doesn't say anything else as he starts jogging with me on his back. I'm impressed he has the stamina after last night. I try to keep my thoughts on last night, but all I can think about going home means going to where his wife and kids live.

I'm a horrible, horrible person.

"We're almost there."

I hear the buzzing of the helicopter before we reach the

clearing, and my heart flutters. I didn't realize that I was anxious about getting out of here until now. I almost died. Only now am I safe.

Enzo's helicopter comes into view, and Langston carries me on. We both settle into the back seat. Beckett sits up front next to Enzo.

"You two both okay? Any injuries we need to take care of right away?" Beckett shouts over the whirling blades.

"No, we're good. Just get us home," Langston answers.

We both grab a pair of headsets as the helicopter takes off.

"Press this button, and you will talk to me only." Langston points to a red button on the headset. "Use this button to talk to everyone." He points to a blue button.

I press the blue button. "Thank you both for saving us."

"We were worried sick. I'm glad you called; we had no idea where you went," Enzo says.

"A Mr. Rowan Wells had us. He was after the treasure," Langston says.

"We have a team out ready to take them out. He won't be a problem again," Enzo says.

Langston looks at me and pushes the button that allows only the two of us to speak to each other. "You should sleep." He holds out his arms, indicating that I can sleep on his lap if I want.

I yawn. I should sleep. But I want to get a few things straightened out first.

"What are we going to do when we get back?"

Langston fidgets with the cord connected to his headset. "I don't know exactly. What I do know is we need to start working together as far as the treasure goes. We can decide who gets it or how to split it later, but if we are going to be attacked constantly, we are stronger together."

I nod, agreeing. "So, where do we start?"

Langston stares at me a moment, considering his answer. "Peru."

"Peru?"

"That's all my side said. To start the search in Peru."

"Where exactly in Peru? Peru doesn't give us a whole lot to go off of."

"The only other clue was cut off. The letters 'tayt' and then the rest was smudged. I assume we start in Machu Pichu and go from there. It's the most famous place in all of Peru."

"No, it's Ollantaytambo. My half had the letters 'Ollan.' It's an Inca town in the Sacred City."

He nods excitedly. We just worked together to figure out where to start. We now have three of the clues from the paper. The city to start in. That others will be searching. And that to get the treasure, you must be married. Langston is. I'm not.

"I need to find someone to marry. That will double our odds of being able to get the treasure."

Langston shakes his head viciously. "No, you aren't getting married."

I roll my eyes. "You're not the boss of me. And you're married. I should be too. That's what's in the note."

"We'll discuss it later," Langston says, switching off his headset and placing it on the hook.

I sigh and take mine off. *One step forward, two steps back.*

I lean back and try to close my eyes to get some sleep, but there is no use. I'm infuriated with Langston. I keep my eyes closed, though, hoping I'll fall asleep eventually. Slumber never comes with Langston snoring next to me.

"Hello," I hear Enzo say faintly from the front. "Yes, I have them." I realize he must be taking a call from Kai.

I smile. I'm jealous of their relationship. It wasn't always easy for them, but it was always clear to everyone around them how right they were for each other, even when I was trying to steal Enzo away for myself.

"Yes, our plan worked."

My ears perk up at that. *Plan? What plan?*

"They were gossiping like two schoolgirls and batting eyelashes at each other. I think they are a bit grouchy from lack of sleep. But yes, Rowan said they were willing to die for one another, that they loved one another. They're planning on working together from now on."

I can't believe I'm hearing this. I open my eyes the tiniest of bits to look over at Langston, but he's still sound asleep.

It was a setup—all of it. They hired Rowan and his team to pretend to kidnap us so Langston and I would be forced to work out our problems.

I'm pissed. I can't believe they played us like that. Unfortunately, there is nothing I can do about it until we land.

—————

"We need to make a quick stop here to refuel; then we'll take you on to your house, Langston," Enzo says before he hops out. Beckett follows, and they both head inside a hangar.

I turn to Langston. "We were set up."

He yawns. "What are you talking about?"

"Rowan was hired by Enzo and all of your supposed friends to try and push us together."

He huffs. "You aren't serious."

"I am. I overheard Enzo talking to Kai on the phone while you were sleeping."

"You heard over the sound of the rotor blades while Enzo was talking into his headset?" He raises his eyebrows in disbelief.

"Yes."

"They would hire someone to kidnap us, torture us, and threaten to kill us—why?"

"Because they are sick of us fighting and playing games like the sex yacht. They thought if we went through a life-threatening ordeal together, it would bring us closer together."

It worked. We did.

For a second, I think Langston is going to believe me. Then he blinks rapidly and runs his hand through his hair. "That's crazy."

"Crazy as me pretending to kill your best friend?"

He narrows his eyes at me.

"Look!" I point into the small hanger that Enzo and Beckett entered. There is a man standing with them for only a second. A man in a suit with sharp-looking hair. He laughs with them then disappears down a hallway.

"That was Rowan," Langston growls.

"See! I told you they schemed against us."

"Well, let's have a little fun in return." He smirks.

I smile along with him. "What do you have in mind?"

Langston climbs into the front seat and pops a compartment open, pulling out a gun. He hands it to me and then pulls his own gun from his waistband. "Let's go get justice for our kidnapping."

My eyes widen. "We aren't really going to kill Rowan, are we?"

"No, but Enzo and Beckett will think we are going to."

I smile, liking this plan. "I just wish Kai, Siren, and Zeke were here to see us."

He thinks a moment. "I think I can arrange that."

I have no idea what he has planned, but I trust him.

Dammit, I trust him. I trust him with everything, even after our quarrel. No matter if their methods were fucked up, their plan worked. Langston and I are a lot closer now.

We walk casually out of the helicopter with our guns in hand. Enzo and Beckett aren't paying us any attention as we stroll to the back of the building. Langston pops a door open and holds his gun out. I follow him doing the same, even though I feel like my gun is for show more than anything else. We already know I won't kill anyone.

We sneak down the hallway before popping into a room where we find Rowan chatting with a pilot.

"Don't move," Langston says, aiming the gun at him.

Rowan freezes with terror in his eyes. "Now, calm down. We should talk about things."

"Talk about what? How you tortured and threatened to kill us? You're not walking out of here alive," I say.

Rowan's face turns pale.

"Mr. Black, will you come in here and explain things a moment?" Rowan shouts.

"You don't want Enzo. He'll kill you right away, while I plan on killing you slowly."

Enzo and Beckett round the corner. To their credit, they don't give anything away. They assess the situation and wait to see what we will do.

"Who is this man?" Enzo asks.

"The man who kidnapped and tortured us," I say.

Rowan's eyes dart to Enzo for help.

"Put your hands behind your back, Rowan," Langston says.

He complies.

"Here, tie him up with these, Liesel. And if you move an inch while she ties you up, I'll shoot you in the balls," Langston orders.

Rowan tenses but keeps his hands behind his back while I tie him up.

Langston trains his gun on his head as he grabs him by the arm and leads him out of the building.

"Not here, Langston. Let's get him back to headquarters, then we can take care of him," Enzo says. It's the first thing he says that gives him away. Enzo takes care of business wherever and whenever. He doesn't need to wait and do it back at headquarters.

Langston nods as he leads Rowan into the back of the helicopter. I hop in the front, and then Langston hops into the pilot's seat before Enzo and Beckett can make it to us. He starts the engine, and then we are taking off.

I should be thinking about how betrayed I was by people who used to be my friends, but all I can think about is how good Langston looks flying a helicopter.

Langston laughs, reading my face as Rowan moans like he's been shot or something behind us.

"Will you shut up?" I say.

"Don't kill me. Mr. Black was the one who hired me. It was all a game to try and get you two closer together. It was for your own good. I hardly touched you two. I gave you a couple of bruises and Langston a dislocated shoulder. I just did what Mr. Black told me to do," he quivers.

"We know," we both say with smug smiles.

"So, you aren't going to kill me?"

"No, but they don't know that. We'll let them think you are drowning in the middle of the ocean."

He laughs. "And where will you hide me?"

Langston winks at me. "In the middle of the fucking ocean." He presses a button, and the side door opens, then he flys the helicopter sideways until Rowan falls out the door and splashes down in the water.

A phone lights up in front of us, and Langston answers. "Yes?"

"Turn the fuck back around," Enzo says.

"Why would I do that?"

"The man you just kidnapped works for me. He's a good man. He has a daughter. Don't kill him."

"His blood is on your hands. You fucking set us up, had us tortured, and thought it was for the best. I don't want to see your face, or you'll end up with a black eye and the inability to have more kids."

"Where is he?" Enzo huffs.

"The middle of the ocean, just like Liesel and I had to endure. Except I tied his hands behind his back instead of the front. You better hope he's a good swimmer." Then Langston hangs up.

"That was cruel."

"You disapprove?"

"No. It was cruel, but definitely deserved."

"You know we have more in common than just being good lays?"

I smile at the twinkle in his eye. Maybe there's a chance yet of one more fuck.

27

LANGSTON

I PUT the helicopter down near my place on a field by the beach. I turn the engine off and then turn to Liesel. In a matter of minutes, we are going to have to deal with the real world.

Kai is going to call me to lecture me about hurting Rowan, even though the guy got a lot less than he deserved. A few minutes in the cool ocean water is nothing compared to what we dealt with at his hands. I don't care who hired him; he's still an asshole. We'll have to deal with Phoenix and possibly explain our relationship to my kids.

But we can put off the inevitable for a few more moments.

We attack each other at the exact same time, so quickly that Liesel still has her seatbelt on and gets pulled back as she grabs for my neck.

I laugh and unbuckle her before I pull her hard across the seat and onto my lap. I grab her neck and kiss her lips with everything I've been holding back since I woke her up with coffee this morning.

"I thought we were done. I thought you wanted nothing to do with me," she says hungrily between kisses.

"I'll never be done with you, huntress. Even if there comes a day when I can't kiss you like this, I'll never be done with you."

I hike her shirt up as my hands run over her smooth skin, trying to memorize everything.

No, I won't be so defeated. Why shouldn't we keep fucking? We are two consenting adults, who—

"Fucking heaven," I groan as Liesel's hands work their way down my pants.

She sucks on my bottom lip with a smirk to her eyes.

"Ever done it in a helicopter?" she squeals.

I shake my head.

After that, everything becomes frantic. Our hands, our mouths, our eyes. Mine work on her pants as hers work my mouth. Then she's unbuttoning my pants, while I'm pushing up her shirt.

I take her nipple in my mouth too roughly, but I love the sharp intake of breath. She retaliates by gripping my cock just a little too hard. But that's how it is between us—a wicked fight that leaves us both with more pleasure than we deserve.

At the same time, I grab her hips as she slides down on my cock.

"God, I've missed you."

"You had me less than five hours ago, and you can have me—"

"Langston?" Phoenix says.

Liesel freezes in my arms, trying to hide, run, anything to not be here right now. Meanwhile, my cock, and even a sliver of my heart, can't let her go.

I don't look at Phoenix. I look at Liesel. Phoenix I know how to deal with, but Liesel I have no idea.

"Give us a minute, Dunn," I say to Phoenix before real-izing my mistake—Dunn is also Liesel's last name.

Liesel rips herself off of me, and I've never felt so bare.

She throws open the door and takes off before I even have my pants up.

I jump out of the helicopter after her, not sure what to do. When I hear Phoenix shouting after me, I don't stop.

I have to talk to Liesel.

But then I hear laughter that makes me stop—my kids.

28

LIESEL

I RUN, not because I'm afraid of Phoenix. Not because I care what she has to say, but because of what Langston will say or do. I can't be here to witness him choosing her over me. I'm a strong woman, but I can't handle that.

I'll have to go back eventually and talk to him, but I won't until after he's greeted his wife.

His wife.

How could I be so stupid?

I sit down on the sand, staring out at the ocean. My flannel shirt and sweatpants are going to be too warm to sit out here in the sun too long, but I just need a little time to let my heart settle.

I hear Langston approaching a second later.

My heart spurs to life, happy that he is choosing me over her. *But maybe it's just to let me down first before he leaves me and grovels to her?*

"It's okay. You can go talk to her. Things can go back to how they were before. We will stop the fighting, stop trying to rip each other apart. We'll just find the treasure and stop people from coming after us. I'll go stay at Siren and Zeke's. I need to thank them for going along with my scheme and see if they were involved with Enzo and Kai's plan."

He sits down next to me as I ramble.

I guess we are doing this now.

"Tell me how you feel, Liesel. The truth."

"We don't have to keep telling the truth to each other. That was before; things are different now. I can lie to you."

"You won't."

"How do you know?"

"I just do."

I can't tell him how I feel because I don't even know. But I can offer him a bit of truth that has been eating at me—another problem we have to solve.

"I don't know how I feel or what you and I should do next. Date? Keep fucking? Become your mistress?"

He winces at the last one. "I would never ask you to be my mistress. Phoenix means nothing to me, not like Waylon meant to you."

My eyes meet his gaze. "Waylon didn't mean what you think he meant to me."

He frowns. "I saw you mourn his death. You fell apart. You cried for the first time in years. You arranged to fake my best friend's death to hurt me back. Don't tell me that Waylon meant nothing to you."

"Waylon was blackmailing me."

He tilts his head, and his eyes plead for that to be true, revealing a hint of his true feelings. Langston wants me for himself. He doesn't want me to have been taken by another man, even a dead man.

"He was blackmailing me—forcing me to play the part of his fiancée and eventually wife in order to find the whereabouts of my son. After Kai returned him to his adopted parents when I refused to see him, thinking he was better off with his adoptive parents, I changed my mind. I wanted to check up on him, but when I went to the adoptive parents' address, they were gone. I searched, but I couldn't find any sign of them.

"And then I met Waylon. He had the information I needed. Once we were properly married, he'd tell me what happened to my son."

"You didn't love Waylon?"

"No, I didn't love him. I thought he was a horrible man, but he was the only person who could tell me what happened to my son."

We hear the kids playing in the sand, then Phoenix's voice telling them not to go near the water.

"It seems you and I were always destined to be with others. You made a good choice in Phoenix. She seems like a loyal person and loving mother. I'm happy for you. Last night was nice, but it's time to go back to reality. You belong with Phoenix, and I belong—"

"We are fated to be together. That's how I've always felt, and you've always fought it. I don't know if we are still destined to be together, but I do know something that might change your mind."

"Honestly, Langston, I don't think I can be with any man right now. I need to focus on finding my son." *Besides, I already know my fate is to be alone.*

"I can help in that department."

"What do you mean?" my heart skips.

"I can help you find your son."

I shake my head. "I've already had everyone's help. No one could find him."

"That's because I didn't want them to know. I didn't want him found until I was ready to tell you."

"Langston, do you know where my son is?"

"Yes." He tilts his head toward his two kids playing in front of us. "He's right in front of you."

———

Thank you so much for reading Fated Lies! Langston & Liesel's story continues in Cruel Lies!

JOIN ELLA's NEWSLETTER & NEVER MISS A SALE OR NEW RELEASE → ellamiles.com/freebooks

Haven't read **Enzo and Kai's story** yet?
I should have run away, found a new life, and started over.
Instead, I returned.
To find the man who sold me.
One-click Taken by Lies for FREE >

Haven't read **Zeke and Siren's story** yet?

She saved me. And now, seeing her about to be sold to the highest bidder, it's my turn to save her.

One-click Sinful Truth for FREE >

Love swag boxes & signed books?
SHOP MY STORE → store.ellamiles.com

Grab Maybe: The Complete Series Here

Grab Definitely: The Complete Series Here

Grab Aligned: The Complete Series Here

Grab Unforgivable: The Complete Series Here

Stolen by Truths #4

Possessed by Lies #5

Consumed by Truths #6

DIRTY SERIES:

Dirty Obsession

Dirty Addiction

Dirty Revenge

Dirty: The Complete Series

ALIGNED SERIES:

Aligned: Volume 1 (Free Series Starter)

Aligned: Volume 2

Aligned: Volume 3

Aligned: Volume 4

Aligned: The Complete Series Boxset

UNFORGIVABLE SERIES:

Heart of a Thief

Heart of a Liar

Heart of a Prick

Unforgivable: The Complete Series Boxset

MAYBE, DEFINITELY SERIES:

Maybe Yes

Maybe Never

Maybe Always

Definitely Yes

Definitely No

Definitely Forever

STANDALONES:

Pretend I'm Yours

Pretend We're Over

Finding Perfect

Savage Love

Too Much

Not Sorry

Hate Me or Love Me: An Enemies to Lovers Romance Collection

ABOUT THE AUTHOR

Ella Miles writes steamy romance, including everything from dark suspense romance that will leave you on the edge of your seat to contemporary romance that will leave you laughing out loud or crying. Most importantly, she wants you to feel everything her characters feel as you read.

Ella is currently living her own happily ever after near the Rocky Mountains with her high school sweetheart husband. Her heart is also taken by her goofy five year old black lab who is scared of everything, including her own shadow.

Ella is a USA Today Bestselling Author & Top 50 Bestselling Author.

Stalk Ella at:
www.ellamiles.com
ella@ellamiles.com